The War is Over

The War is Over

stories by

Hugh Underhill

To Angela
and many more years of friendship!
Hugh

Hugh Underhill

Shoestring Press

Typeset and printed by Q3 Print Project Management Ltd, Loughborough, (01509) 213456

Published by Shoestring Press
19 Devonshire Avenue, Beeston, Nottingham, NG9 1BS
Telephone: (0115) 925 1827
www.shoestringpress.co.uk

First published 2005
© Copyright: Hugh Underhill
The moral right of the author has been asserted.
ISBN: 1 904886 22 1

Shoestring Press gratefully acknowledges financial assistance from
Arts Council England

In Memory of Arthur Underhill
1906–2003

and for his daughters
Pam, Valerie and Jackie

Acknowledgements

'Mrs Permanently' appeared in *Chrysalis* (1993); 'The Old Kodak' in *Rivet* (1995); 'Missing' and 'Homecoming' in *The Interpreter's House* (1996, 1998), 'One Morning in March 1960' in *the magazine* (1999); 'Aunt Penelope' in *Staple* (2000); 'Amor Platonicus' in *Writer's Muse* (2002). 'The Visit' was highly commended in *Raconteur* competition 1993; 'Gingerbread Hearts' in Swanage Festival competition 1995. 'Monica' won first prize in the Basingstoke Short Story Competition 1992.

Contents

Missing

It was the end of the line, and the trains came slinking into the platforms, long green reptiles with squashed flat faces, and eased up to the buffers. People started coming, first in ones and twos, then in a flood, and finally again in odd ones or two. They banked up behind the ticket barrier and were let through like little bursts of air out of a balloon.

He watched hard. He was searching for a tall, slightly stooping figure, for a face he couldn't quite get clear in his mind but which he was sure he would recognise as soon as he saw it.

His father had never come back at the end of the war. There were other fathers, of course, who didn't come back, but a lot more did. He knew that there were two "ends" to the war, one early and one late in that summer. The first was when the Germans surrendered; that was when the pictures were in the papers of the generals round a table, in what looked like some kind of tent, signing things. It was an "unconditional" surrender, whatever that meant; words like that stuck in your head. The second was following all the pictures of the mushroom cloud from the atom bomb. Its swelling feathery shape was especially spectacular on the cinema newsreel. Then, the Japanese surrendered too.

Before the first, you had already been allowed to go on the beach again. He could hardly remember the summers before the beaches closed, but now the mines had been cleared, and he and other children ran across the sands on their way home from school. One afternoon, out on the horizon, trails of brown smoke rose above the sea. People were looking; somebody said that ships must be firing flares. And somebody else shouted: "The war must be over!" The news hopped along among the little bunches of people on the sands. Soon, sure enough, a man had just heard it on the wireless: "The war is over!"

The tide was a long way out and the sun gleamed on the expanses of wet sand. Near where the sea broke in miniature waves, the sand was formed into a network of perfect ripples. He liked putting his bare foot across the little sand-ridges, so that he could watch the print it left, pale and dry-looking for the first second or two, then slowly going dark and watery.

The months went by and his father made no appearance. Not that anything was different, because his father hadn't been there for a long time anyway.

Sometimes he was sent to Sunday School. The children were told stories by a lady who seemed to want to be nice but couldn't quite manage it. He hated the bits about hammering in the nails, and couldn't bear to look at the carving in the church with the blood trickling all over Jesus's hands and feet and forehead and gushing out of his side, but he listened carefully to what was said about Jesus coming again.

Somebody said to him once, was his father "missing"? He said he didn't know, and when he went home asked his mother. No, she said, his father wasn't missing, but he wasn't actually coming back. She seemed a bit cross, and started talking about something else.

Then one day she put on his best clothes, the ones he usually went to church in, and took him to the railway station. He held on to her hand while she led him to a place just by the bookstall, and told him to stand there. Don't move on any account, she said. And she let go his hand and disappeared. He saw her for a moment going towards the big glass doors leading to the booking office, but then she was gone. He stood as he'd been told. After a couple of minutes the tall stooping man with the face he knew appeared in front of him. They had a very nice day, though it was sometimes a bit strange, his father didn't quite know what to do with him. But he was very nice all the same, and they spent a long time in the toyshop. When it was time to go home, after the ice-creams and the toyshop, he was taken back to the station bookstall and told again not to move on any account. His father disappeared through the barrier onto the platform. Then after a few minutes he saw his mother returning from the direction of the booking office.

This happened twice. Nobody explained. His mother muttered something about his father not wanting to see her any more. This was strange. There was a time, he could remember it exactly, when his mother and father used to see each other every day. They even used to see each other without any clothes. But now they wouldn't see each other at all, even with their clothes on.

What was clear, though, what one had to realize about his father, was that he could come and go, appear and disappear, at any time. Even his mother didn't seem to grasp this. But he was sure to turn up again at the station sooner or later. So when you got a bit bigger, big enough to go out that far by yourself, that was the place you had to go and wait for him. You watched the long green trains sidling into the platforms, the doors swinging open, some before the train had even stopped, people shooting out and rushing towards the barrier in a terrific hurry, others slowly climbing down onto the platform with loaded suitcases.

It was true that you had to do a lot of waiting. But then it wasn't boring, there was always something going on at the station, and anyway there was a lot of time, from one summer holiday to another, from one Christmas to the next.

These were immense tracts of time through which his small life progressed along its fixed track with barely perceptible motion, but he was quite sure that one day his father would come again.

Monica

An old man materialized inside the glassed-in verandah. He peered through the glass; I held up the envelopes. He pointed to a path round to the back, so I went. One of a row of doors looked used and had a letter-box in it, but before I could push the envelopes through, the door opened.

"Ah ... thankyou postman ..." Looking at the envelopes in the slow-motion way some old people have, tilting them towards the light.

The top of his head was on a level with my chin. He was partly bald, his face and hands were dark and wrinkled, like the skin of a ripe passion-fruit. He wore that durable clothing from the days when people patched and mended and passed things on.

"Oh ... you're just for Christmas, are you? Well ... bring the post round the side here, will you? The front doors are stuck, you know."

A few minutes later I saw him from the end of the lane where it curved round and became beach-sand and pebbles. Because of the curve one could look along the back of the line of makeshift bungalows converted from disused pre-war railway carriages; the old man was carrying a white enamel bowl to the end of his miniature plot of garden. I saw him tip the contents – from the dust which puffed up they must have been ashes – into a ditch between his garden and the flat winter fields. Somewhere out in the fields there was the steady sound of a tractor at work.

I was filling in with the Christmas post, as you always could then if you were a student or, like me, in-between things. There were two deliveries on weekdays and I'd finished them both by about half-past three in the afternoon, when I met Monica. She slipped out for half-an-hour from the office where she worked and we had a cup of tea in the cafeteria of Staley's Department Store. It was warm in there, steam rising from the counter, from one of those big hissing tea-urn things, all taps and valves. You don't see them any more.

I'm trying to remember what Monica was like. I know that whenever we walked anywhere the sort of high-heeled shoes girls wore in those days clicked sharply on the pavement and the curls permed into her hair brushed the side of my face.

I told her about the old man. "Looks to me a bit of a weird old character."

"Perhaps he's got skeletons in the cupboard!" She made a silly sort of mock-fearful moan.

"More likely a mattress stuffed with dirty ten-bob notes."

Her gaze drifted up into the high ceiling of the cafeteria, which had an array of pipes running across it. They were painted white in a futile effort at disguise, and I supposed were to do with the heating and plumbing of our town's largest store.

"Do you think he'll be lonely at Christmas?" She looked back at me with exaggerated melancholy. Monica was always bothering about people being lonely at Christmas. If you were going to be lonely, I couldn't quite see what difference Christmas made.

A few days later there was a violent stormy morning. It was still blowing hard when I got to the lane, some way out of the town, where the old man lived: fallen branches and other debris were scattered around. Anybody who grew up in the sort of sea-side place I did may know of these curiosities, clusters of little dwellings knocked up out of old train carriages, wheels gone and stood on blocks, their cambered rooves and rows of windows remaining among the trimmings and adornments. They had their own little gardens and front fences. I suppose they'd been intended, some time between the wars, for holidaying, but now many of them seemed permanent homes. I don't know whether any are still there – they'd be in a kind of time-warp now. The old man was standing outside, shrugging himself up into a rough khaki-coloured cardigan, his hands in his pockets, but apparently not much bothered by the weather. He watched me coming and I handed him a single envelope. He seemed to mutter something but a skirl of wind got between us.

"I'm sorry, I didn't hear," I shouted.

"I said, are you a student?"

"Not exactly."

"Oh."

The bloodshot eyes in the dark wrinkled face peered at me a moment, either short-sightedly or piercingly – I couldn't tell. I thought he was going to ask me *what* exactly and was glad he didn't, because I didn't know either. He turned up the half-waterlogged path toward his section of immobilised train. But just as I was pushing off on the antiquated bike the post-office had allocated me I heard a plop and a sort of grunt behind me. He had slipped and was kneeling with one knee and the palm of one hand glued in the mud. Later, in Staley's, I told Monica how I had helped him up and he hadn't seemed much the worse for it, only repeatedly telling me that I must get on and not fuss with him.

Monica had decided we had to go that evening to a Christmas carol concert in the parish church. I was beginning to find Monica irritatingly sentimental, and to wonder why I was continuing to let her have some kind of hold over me. We sat on the hard seats in the undistinguished late-Victorian nave and listened to the local church choir and organist. About half-way through the proceedings I thought I spotted him in the side aisle on the other side of the church. He was in front at the sort of angle at which it's hard to make people out, especially in the shadowy lighting which had been laid on for atmosphere. I nudged Monica and tried to make her understand in whispers and gestures that it was him. She spent the rest of the concert staring hard at the wrong people and going through a facial pantomime, trying to get more exact directions from me.

The music ended and as people began to eddy towards the doors Monica hung back to get a closer look at him. But just as he had started shambling along the opposite aisle and I was sure it was him, the vicar detached himself from a huddle of his flock and laid a hand on the old man's arm.

The relationship which existed between the vicar and myself had been established since my desertion of the faith at the age of fourteen. Whenever he caught sight of me he headed toward me holding out the laying-on hand and his lips forming some salutation. I promptly took evasive action. Blatant as this was, it never deterred him; the same sequence took place every time we came within view of each other. Now, before I could hurry Monica up, they were both staring across at me as they talked – and I must have been the subject of that talk. I abandoned Monica and in a few seconds was out of the church and in shadow on the other side of the road.

Monica was piqued, of course, when she caught me up, and made us stand there until he appeared, alone, in the lighted church porch. We followed some way behind him down the street past Staley's with its decorated windows and round the corner to the bus station. At night the bus station had strange green lighting which when I was a child had always turned it for me into an eerie cavern, into which the double-deck buses swayed ponderously. It made faces look ghostly. He stood there under the lighting, crouched up inside his shabby coat with hands in his pockets, his old face bleached green, until his bus came.

Nobody was in when we got to Monica's place so we went up to her room and got under the eiderdown and got warm and fondled. The convention was that secluded under that covering some limited unbuttoning and feeling around was permitted. That was as far as things ever seemed to go in those unliberated days of the fifties. She began an elaborate fantasy about how we would go and pay a visit to the old man on Christmas Eve. We would take a present of some kind, she couldn't quite think what.

At midnight, I was put out into the squeaking frost.

We never went, of course, and Monica seemed to forget about him until we saw a paragraph in the local paper on New Year's Eve. He had died on Christmas Day. We knew it was him because I remembered his name from the mail I'd delivered. He'd been found in a chair by a grate of cold ashes, it said in the paper. A few words were quoted from my old sparring-partner the vicar, about the sad passing of so worthy and long-standing a member of the congregation, etc. Monica said she just had to go and see his place now, so on New Year's Day we went. It had snowed lightly and thawed again and the air was leaden and dank. The place seemed to have fallen suddenly into much worse decay in the week since I had seen it. It looked about ready to collapse. We went and tried the glass door in the verandah and the door round at the back but of course they were locked, or jammed. We glared hard through the glass but all we could see was the same old junk I'd seen there before. Monica said she could see some Christmas cards on a table or something but I couldn't honestly make anything out, it was too dark inside.

I began to worry that somebody would report us for snooping, and tried to get Monica away. I don't know what she expected to find.

We went along the lane to the sea. The usual winter litter and flotsam were strewn about on the beach. Monica picked up a smooth green pebble and shone it between her gloves, then held it up to try to see through it. She gave it to me and I looked, but it wasn't the translucent kind. It *was* very smooth between your fingers. Then it slipped from my grasp and as it fell – I was shuffling my feet aimlessly about – I accidentally scuffed sand over it.

We were going to look for it again and then didn't.

The sea was grey in the calm sunless afternoon and tight little waves broke on the beach. We stood about getting chilled until a thin reddish tint spread through the haze at the horizon and a few lights went on in the train-carriages behind us. Monica and I hardly saw each other after that and I wrote away for jobs. I didn't much mind what the job was.

Gingerbread Hearts

"*Meine Damen und Herren!*"
A few heads turn in the direction of the interruption. A little man takes an incongruously huge step forward among the tables, opening his arms wide.

"A small entertainment!"

The odd-looking couple has come in from the street just as a brisk waitress puts Calder's beer on the table in front of him. This little thin man in a seedy evening suit and bow-tie, with a pointed nose, fowl-like eyes under thick eyebrows, greasily flattened grey hair, and a meticulous manner; a gypsy-looking woman in a long many-coloured dress, a shawl over her head and shoulders, a basket on her arm.

The woman puts her basket on the floor; they both fumble in it, heads down and tails up like chicken pecking corn. Six or seven white balls. The man steps back with them into the middle of the room, erects his little grey-haired figure to give it a cock-of-the-walk stance, and repeats:

"*Meine Damen und Herren!* A small entertainment!"

He juggles with the balls. He throws one ball higher than the others, bends forward, catches the ball in the back of his neck, and lets it roll down his back into an upturned hand held behind him like a scrawny tail.

"*Danke, meine Damen und Herren.*" He bows, but there is no applause. "Now – something different!"

He gives the white balls back to the woman. The barman and waitresses pay no attention. Now he holds some silver-painted cardboard rings which the woman has fished from the basket. The man's tinny voice with incongruous bravura:

"Something different, *meine Damen und Herren!*"

And he begins to juggle with the silver rings.

Slumming his way around the Continent all those years ago, this night in particular imprinted itself on Calder's memory. Polishing his language skills, that had been the pretext. If you weren't choosy jobs were easy then, the post-war economies still building up. He took casual jobs here and there, and a rented room, or put up in a hostel.

He can hear, above the hubbub among the tables, some kind of dance music. It's coming from an opening at the back into another room. But now it's stopped, and a few people squash into the opening to watch. In his tired and depressed state he must have started seeing apparitions. A glistening girl's face appears between the shoulders of two tall youths. She seems to be standing on tiptoe, straining to see the juggler.

He starts to get up. But all at once, the place has gone still, faces at all the tables turned towards the shabby old cockerel going on in great style, even the waitresses gliding silently.

"*So, meine Damen und Herren*, I hope the small entertainment pleased you. Thankyou for your very kind attention!"

The little cockerel bowing grandly; a metal plate passed across to him by the woman. He goes to a far corner, people put a coin or two on the plate. It's painful how slowly he works his way round to where Calder sits. Calder, too, drops in his couple of Marks. The scratched elderly voice thanks him, the little stooping cockerel on the point of pecking from his table, so deferential. Can't he get it over with?

At last the couple packs up; the room forgets them before they have even gone through the door. Trying to look casual, Calder strolls across to the back opening. The space is dim, airless and smoky. Hardly room for a dozen dancers, but small-town musicians pump heavy rhythms for the youths and girls in cramped motion on the floor. He peers through the smoke, people beginning to notice him.

What could he have been expecting to find? What a state of bemusement he must have been in! It was totally impossible she could be there. Only a few hours earlier he had left her wiping her eyes at Frankfurt *Hauptbahnhof*.

She'd been packed off to relatives in Frankfurt to get her out of his way, but he'd followed her down there. They found ways to meet a few times, then that, too, was discovered and made impossible. The reasons for it all were mystifying. It was another place, another time, where codes operated which made him a quite unacceptable suitor.

He took the train back to Cologne, and never saw her again. For many years he continued to think of her as his great lost chance. But with time it had grown impossible to be sure …

The glistening girl in the back room, of course, was as much of a phantasm as the Lorelei maiden who haunted the legendary rock a few miles down the river. How sorry for himself he had felt! There were several hours to go before the first early-morning train from this place where he'd mistakenly broken his journey.

He sinks down again into his seat, orders another beer, tries to take his mind off things by watching people around him.

All these people filling the cavernous old room of the *Wirtschaft* can't be in his own fix. Most of them must have beds to go to. But they seem intent on staying out of them.

These two, for instance. A man so lean and attenuated that he sits arched over a table like a drooping plant, his holiday clothes dangling from him like dying leaves, depleted hair smoothed with oil (faint perfume washing Calder's way) but with one lock falling in a sickle over his forehead. He winds a tendril of an arm about a much younger woman, contrastingly squat and shapeless. Her expressionless face is conspicuous only for a bright blossom of lipstick and eyes heavily shaded in blue. The man speaks to her continuously in a low voice; she never replies, but every few minutes the lipstick-blossom meets the man's mouth as his head droops towards hers.

But surely those two young girls, sitting with a woman just over there, should be in bed by this time?

The younger is about twelve, the elder perhaps fifteen. It penetrates Calder's fatigue that the elder sister's eyes are steadily on him. Blue eyes, cool and unreflecting. He meets them with the silent contact she has willed. She holds his eyes wilfully before returning to desultory talk with the others.

She's a robust, ordinary sort of girl, but newly aware, he guesses, of her powers. The mother is herself no more, perhaps, than a dozen years older than Calder, with a sort of comfortable plumpness and gently indolent face. *Her* eyes pass with lazy knowingness between him and the girl.

For half-an-hour he is silently possessed by the girl and her mother, the younger daughter unheeding and sleepy. All the time they sip drinks and talk drowsily among themselves. Then the three of them rise, gather handbags, tidy themselves with quick little strokes of the hand. They pass him towards the door. The woman turns her half-smile with a lazy directness on him as she goes. The girl steers close to him, brushing his arm with her skirt, and walks as if naked into the night.

He must have sat there as long as he could, still with a faint sense of that brushing on his arm. Then the place started to close, and he had to force himself up from his seat. The smell of cigar-smoke hung stickily in the street outside. There were moments for long afterwards when that smell, in abrupt coldness of air, would suddenly return to him. People drifted about the narrow alleys, across which upper storeys with elaborate carved woodwork nearly touched. A couple of drunks rolled from side to side, wailing some song in which he caught the words "*Heimatlos and verlassen*" – "homeless and forsaken". Calder walked on in what he thought was the direction of the railway station.

Did he come this way before? It's a part of the town he doesn't recognise. The streets are deserted, except for a man lighting a cigarette, apparently watching him. It seems best to ask the way.

"I'll walk with you. I'm going that way," says the man.

What a pissing nuisance! Calder is too tired to make conversation, let alone in German.

There isn't much light and he can't see the stranger very clearly. The man keeps asking questions, in the formal German way, where does Calder come from, why is he here, that kind of thing. But he seems interested and sympathetic. "*Mein Gott!* The *Winzerfest!* Of all nights in the year to stop off here without somewhere booked!"

Also, he praises Calder's German, too much. It isn't *that* good. Then he points the way, as they stop at a corner.

"Just along this street, at the end, you come to the station."

They are under a street-lamp now, pale light the colour of lemonade. The stranger seems to be staring into Calder's face.

"My flat isn't far from here. There won't be any trains yet ...." (his eyes flicking away with a hint of awkwardness) "Perhaps you would have time to come and drink some coffee?"

The man has used the intimate "*du*", and has taken Calder's arm. It's as if he is claiming him. He is being possessed for the second time that night. He begins to resist. The man wants to shake hands … he grips Calder's hand hard. He tries to withdraw but the hand hangs on greedily.

It was like the struggle to surface at the end of a dream, he thought afterwards.

A sharp fingernail runs across his palm, and at the same time, in the darkness, this stranger's other hand moves with only slight hesitation between Calder's legs.

He mutters something, pulls free. *We all have our needs*, he's confusedly thinking, *but I can't* …. And hurrying away, he stubs his foot against some object on the ground. Stooping to look at it in the dawn light, he finds a broken half of a gingerbread heart, and kicks the stupid thing into the gutter. A pinkish glow is starting above the rim of hills around the town.

The picture-book-looking place on the Rhine had looked inviting that autumn evening. He had got out of the train to find somewhere to stay the night. How could he have known it was *Winzerfest*, the vintage festival, there? The woman in the information office outside the station tapped a pencil hopelessly on the counter. Not a *pension* or hotel room for miles around.

He couldn't get to Cologne at that time of night. What was he to do except wait for the first morning train? And picking his way through a raucous funfair on the riverbank, there they were, the sweet-stalls with the gingerbread hearts. Strung up all round, one row above another, feverish pink icing dribbled over each heart-shaped brown lump: *Ich liebe dich*.

Had she been the love of his life? Certainly, for a long time afterwards, none of the others had seemed quite the same.

My Life as an Automaton

My life as an Automaton didn't last for long. It is also ancient history now; my fellow-automaton Hermann was quite right about how things would change.

"By the eighties, say," he pronounced, "there'll be complete computerisation. And regulations to cut down the stink. Just wait, you see."

Hermann's father had been a schoolteacher over in the East and, as well as the usual communist stuff, he seemed to know all sorts of things. Perhaps that didn't help him to be an automaton. Anyway, I was too preoccupied to look that far ahead, and in the end I didn't wait around to see.

My last day went like this:

I change into my enveloping crisp white oversuit and walk into the great windowless hall lit by glowing white bands in the ceiling. The tribulations of the outer world cannot reach us here. Hermann once said we shelter in here as in a womb. At least, I think that's what he said but my German is not perfect.

I prepare now to thread my first spool. It is a skilled manoeuvre; the thread must be poised with exactly the right tension on the forefinger and then the series of loops and twists around the rollers and cylinders must be accomplished with swift precision. The machines "stretch" the thread so that it is ready for weaving. One day I made a small misjudgement and in an instant my hand was jerked into the machine. I had to have my fingertip sewn back on at the hospital. Three doctors, no less, attended me. They did a superb job. There is only a slight deformity of the finger now and I am functioning with complete normality.

The hundred machines stand like three military squads; the hum of machinery is multiplied a hundred times, and we automata have to shout at each other constantly to make ourselves heard. It's all right, it helps keep us on our toes. We are all clad in the same brilliant white, three hundred of us. Shift after shift, three every twenty-four hours, we set out the spools, thread the silk through the rollers and cylinders, remove the cones of stretched silk, forty-eight at a time, and start again.

I must work fast. I have thirty minutes to get my first forty-eight spools done but at the beginning of the shift when I'm fresh I can do it in twenty. That leaves ten to go and sit on the floor in the *Toiletten* and glance at the paper and have a cigarette. I have to squeeze between others already there. The smoke from a dozen or so cigarettes smothers the smells from the rows of cubicles. I may stay another five minutes, taking them out of my next forty-eight which I can also do in less than thirty. These breaks are not officially permitted, but as long as each forty-eight is completed within its time-slot the overseers say nothing. Sometimes, though, I lock myself in a cubicle and think about Annelise, and have been known to run over time, when I've been reprimanded.

Annelise and I have to communicate a lot of the time in writing, even though the room I rent is only five minutes walk from her house. I've got a letter from her in my pocket now. I must undo my oversuit to get at it.

"Just imagine, my darling," she has written, "now I'm ill again. I was just about to go to the office, when suddenly and quite crazily the fever came."

She's propped against pillows, it seems, scribbling before her mother returns from shopping. I've got to decipher the German, and I've left my pocket dictionary in my locker in the changing room.

"But perhaps you won't believe I'm really ill."

She's afraid I'll think she's been pressured into pretending sickness, just another ruse to stop us meeting. Her family will go to any lengths. I had thought that sort of thing went out with the Victorians.

"And, of course, the worst of it is that I can't see you this evening."

We always have to be finding new places to meet, often in the wet or freezing cold, until each place is discovered by her parents' network of informers and spies. In a small town where everybody knows everybody, a united front against outsiders is an easy tune to play.

"Oh darling, will you be angry? How can I tell? How can we *really* know each other very well?"

Good question. We are from different countries. When we were children, our countries were at war. And though we met twelve months ago, the difficulties made by everybody around her mean that we have actually been together very little.

At lunch-break to-day I have to try to see Reg. He is one of the automata in grey protective clothing who operate in the part of the factory where the process which immediately precedes "stretching" takes place. It is less skilled work than ours for the fibre is still coarse and thick, and it is not clean and light there as it is with us. But I am sometimes impressed by the way Reg and the others in their heavy grey suits look and move like moonwalkers.

But it's there that the stink is worst. It's caused by the chemicals from which the thread is made melting in a furnace overhead. Night and day this smell permeates the factory and spreads through the surrounding countryside.

Like me, Reg is English. Here in the factory, it's not like in the town. There don't seem any difficulties being a foreigner, even with the war still in everybody's memory. Some of my fellow-automata don't mind talking about Hitler. There was no work, they say, and then came Hitler, and there *was* work. Yes, Hitler was *verrückt*, insane, but what were you to do?

But it seems to me we are a lot more well-off and industrious here than back in England these days and I'm not sure I'm going there again.

Reg certainly won't. He's been in prison there because he married a German woman omitting to divorce his wife in England. His new wife insisted on a honeymoon in England and, of course, they had to renew their passports and one thing led to another. Now he is back here with his German woman and they are trying to start afresh. But he hasn't enough money and because I am an unmarried automaton he thinks I don't need much of my own. But I have to try to get back some of the three thousand Marks I've lent him. I need it to get Annelise away from here so we can be together.

16

However, Reg is an evasive bastard though he pretends to be my friend and I don't quite know how I'm going to get the money out of him. Come to think of it, it's because of Reg that I'm here at all and ever got landed with this problem. He uses me. I may have to go and get advice from the Social Department. They certainly helped me a lot when I was out of action with my damaged hand.

If you work here, everything is provided, cradle to grave. In the Social Department there is a coloured photograph of the Company President and underneath it a message in which he says: "For me the most important thing in our undertaking is the human being engaged in it."

When Hermann went in there one day with me, he stood staring at it and laughed out loud. "I'll tell you what," he said, pointing at himself. "Here's one human being whose arse the President can lick."

That, by the way, is adapting a phrase used constantly around here. One must be able to give it exactly the right vehement intonation and guttural relish, and it is the piece of German which I have perhaps most perfected.

But Hermann needs the job. When he came over from the East he was able to bring nothing with him, and he has a wife and baby.

Twice every day, as I enter the factory and leave it, I pass the old village mill surrounded by willow-trees, where the factory began. It has been preserved, the mill-wheel hanging idly over the mill-stream.

I pass it now at the end of the shift, on my way to the bike-sheds where my second-hand machine is stowed. I didn't get far with Reg.

"Well, you see, old mate ..." Infuriating the way he calls me his old mate. "There's the instalment on the dining suite this week ... the rent coming up again next week. You don't have these sorts of expenses, you don't know what it's like. In a few more weeks, though, I might be seeing some light at the end of the tunnel."

Some bloody tunnel this.

Then, I must have been thinking too much about that because I got a bit behind with my forty-eights and had to rush to catch up. When one automaton gets out of rhythm it messes up all the others and I got bawled at.

Yes, it's been a tiring day. I seem to be lapsing into a dream as I pedal mechanically. I'm thinking of Annelise's letter again. Maybe it was standing with me in the woods in the pouring rain brought back her fever …

Without noticing, I must have swerved too far out into the road. A car clips my front wheel. It's funny, as I go on a weightless spin through the air, with what complete calmness the thought goes through my mind, well, that's the end of *my* problem.

I wake up sitting in the middle of the road with a ring of half-a-dozen people round me. I think the driver of the car is more upset than I am; his hair is positively standing on end and he keeps jerking up and down like some machine in the factory.

As I sit here in the road with the change-of-shift buses looping past me I can see, hazily, the monster factory, huge chimneys smoking in the middle of country fields, over there in the distance. And I can see I've got to get out of its clutches. It is what Hermann would do if he could and if he had anywhere else to go.

The whole affair with Annelise has been most un-automaton-like anyway.

"You're lucky," someone is saying, "getting off so lightly."

He may think so, he hasn't got these cuts and bruises. Still, they'll be an excuse not to go back for the length of my week's notice and then I'll just pick up my wage-packet and Annelise and I will clear out of here. That is, if she'll come, which since I haven't got the money from Reg she probably won't. She's supposed to be engaged to this bloke, some well-heeled local type, she doesn't want to marry. Her family pushed her into it. The plan was that if I could get my three thousand Marks, together with what we've saved, she'd do a flit and we'd both get jobs somewhere else a good way off.

I expect I'll have to go by myself and that'll be that. Reg can keep my money. It won't do him any good, nothing ever does.

He can have this old bike with the buckled front wheel too.

The Visit

"Take my word for it. Family, neighbours, and colleagues out of office-hours," (he enumerates the categories with slight pauses) "have nothing to do with them. It's the only way. They're always wanting to stick their noses in, but it's best not to give them the chance. Their opinions are hardly worth tuppence, their advice is usually wrong, and anyway, it's your own life and you've a right to live it your own way."

It's a precept the old man has stuck to all his life, only getting more stubborn about it with the years. He offers it to me now as a sort of morsel of wisdom for a young visitor. After which, his arms fall slowly back into his lap. His mottled hands mould round the book he has taken automatically from the side of the chair.

Yet ten or so years ago, when he was still running the office, we struck up this odd relationship. He showed a sort of openness with me, not like with any of the other staff. God knows why, but here it is happening again. He's suddenly, for no reason that I can fathom, telling me about the old house he lived in as a boy. He keeps on about its *whiteness*. Nearly two hundred years it had been in the family, and there it still stood. The white was what he remembered. You could easily make it out from a mile or more away up on the hills. Coming home from school for the holidays, long before you got there, you saw its elegant white form taking pride of place in the village in the hollow. It looked across the green with its pond and ducks to *The Rising Sun* on the other side, and beyond, poking above the horse-chestnuts and yews, the squat church tower. Norman with some remnants of Saxon stone. He wonders, is any of that still there? Probably, conserved for the tourist and heritage trade, a little pocket among the motorways and housing estates …

He checks himself. Perhaps he's embarrassed, running on in that way. He doesn't use my name, though I introduced myself when I arrived. I think he's confused whether I'm Smithson or Thompson. There were two of us started at the office in the same week. I suppose he can't be expected to fit the right names to everyone he appointed in all those years.

"Of course," he says, in a changed tone, "I'm letting nostalgia get the better of me. How stupid! I'm the last person needs reminding that things *look* better as they recede into the past. It's human nature, always been the same. The good things are always gone or to come, never now, never here … Well, if that's what people think is true, it *is* a kind of truth. It's what people *want* to think is true, that counts."

He offers this as his second morsel of wisdom to young Smithson, or Thompson, whichever I am.

"Take my word for it. I've been around longer than you."

But now he's off again. It was only the house and its whiteness he'd loved, his childhood wasn't much. To escape his people badgering him to start in the business, he went off and played at being down and out in Paris and several other parts of a troubled Europe. And then there was the war. At thirty, as a junior officer, he found himself capable of a certain detached efficiency. It was nothing to do with heroics, but he could seal himself off and meet crises and organize things. And when he came out of the army, what else was there to do but pick up the pieces in the firm? Pretty rickety it was by then, but he built it up again modestly …

Why is he telling me all this? With him, non-communication is a fine art. He shuts himself away hermit-like down here in this near-hovel, and it's unlike him to feel any need to explain himself. I must be more careful. Perhaps he's noticed me casting a doubtful eye round the place, and feels some urge to justify the contrast with the old house, with his earlier life. Or does he find in me whatever it was he found back then, when he was still at the office? It would be ridiculous, of course, to think he saw in me, even for a moment, the son he never had. Out of all those youngsters that had come and gone over the years!

He married an invalid, never had children. There was only the one niece. Does that intent look on his face mean he's trying to dig out of the back of his mind what's happened to her?

"Yes … nostalgia's a powerful thing!" he mutters, half to himself, half to me.

"My God, what an impossible idyll, the old village green, and all that! I bet you're thinking, how did he end up here? But it was never a real world, do you see, not really. See that cabinet over there? The only thing left from the old house, the only thing I managed to hang on to. Chippendale. Oh yes, you can stare. Thought it was a bit of old junk, didn't you? Well, *that's* the real thing, believe what you like. Worth a bob or two? Certainly. Do you think I'm short of cash, just because I'm cooped up here?"

I know he isn't.

"Ask my relatives – except I'm not going to tell you where they are. You might tell 'em where *I* am! Arnold, he was the worst of them, my elder brother. Got off going into the army in the war, supposed to have been running the firm. Let it fall to pieces … He's the one took most of the stuff from the house, greedy sod."

A sort of half-smile, as if at his own exaggerated vehemence.

"Might be dead and buried by now, for all I know – or care. Seven years older than me, so he probably is. Married a second time, when he already had one foot in the grave. I hardly knew the woman. She must have been daft if she married *him*!"

A brittle chuckle. He fixes cloudy eyes on me. Does this mean I'm to take what he says with a pinch of salt? Actually, I can hardly stop bursting out:

"But of course you know about your brother! You didn't go to the funeral and nobody expected you to, but you were told, through your solicitors, you old nutcase!"

I can't, of course. He shuts himself away down here, and I turn up without any warning. How's he to have any idea that I'm almost one of the family too?

Yet, almost as if he has, he mutters: "There was a little girl …" Then he falls still again. He has this way of switching between fierce animation and apparent exhaustion. He seems almost lifeless now, staring through the window at the winter sunlight. It slants into the dim room. The woodwork's chipped, the wallpaper's stained, and the room smells of age.

Then, after the moment of complete stillness, he fidgets in his chair. His bony face pans slowly round the room. At last, he shifts himself laboriously to the front edge of the seat, and pushes on its arms to raise himself. He pads over to the Chippendale cabinet.

"See this? Look at it! A couple of hundred years old. Worcester porcelain. Chinese sort of decoration, the vogue at that time. Look at the colour – look! When you put it up to the light. That line of gold round the edges. The blue and the red birds. Look at its transparency!"

His hands tremble perilously as they hold the fragile antique up to the window.

"Just a few of these bits left over from the old house, you see."

I do, because I've been shown companion pieces, in the things left by the elder brother when he died. Much of it had to be sold, but Moira got a few oddments.

"Come to that, how did you find your way here? Oh yes, you said. Daft of me telling you, all that time ago. Yes, I remember you. Cocky bastard, you always were. Thought you knew everything. I remember you at my leaving do. What did they have to put that farce on for? Just a last bit of malice, I suppose. And you! Thought you could *hold* your drink, didn't you? Hope that taught you a lesson, but I don't suppose it did."

Whenever a memo landed on his desk or whenever he issued some edict he'd initial it W.O.G. That's how he got his nickname. It was a catch-cry around the place: "Hear what that miserable old fart Wog's done now?" But most of us were sorry when he went. He'd run an efficient outfit, from which we all benefitted. And he'd had his good side, despite acting the old misanthrope. I always wondered about that. I was only twenty then, still studying in the evenings. He let out to me about this ramshackle place down on the coast, a sort of holiday bungalow. He went to it at weekends, he said, and planned to live there when he retired. Nobody else in the office seemed to know about it, and I kept it to myself.

"The water-colours you're looking at? My wife did those. That's the beach at the end of the road there. You must have come that way. She could sell her stuff, you know, from time to time. Doctors said the sea air would do her good. It didn't ..."

A pause, and then he's off again. I don't interrupt. I don't really know what to say.

"That would have been before your time. When was it you came to the office? Not long before I went, was it? Come to think of it, I can remember you and Thompson, or whichever of you is which, going on about things. All that sixties sort of stuff, suppose you were growing up then. You probably thought I wasn't listening. Thought you knew it all, thought you were going to change the world. Instead, it's got worse, hasn't it? That's how it is. Bigotry and envy are what makes the world tick, not the sort of things you were always talking about. I expect I told you so then. It was just a freak, those few years – you see that now, don't you? Always been the same, a little outbreak of sweetness and light – and bang! That's the end of it."

Morsel of wisdom number three. Last I heard, Thompson had some plush job with a multi-national in Australia. Joined the yuppies good and proper.

Then, startlingly, he jerks up to the light again the hand with the antique cup in it.

"Sentimental really, keeping this stuff. All right if you like that sort of thing. My wife did. Better be careful not to drop it, though."

The brittle chuckle. His lean shoulders jerk with it beneath an oversized woollen cardigan. In his days at the office, that cardigan would have fitted.

Christ, his whole body's shaking. His bony finger and thumb twitch where they meet on the wisp of china handle, part slightly, and the cup falls. But he's standing on a tattered bit of deep-pile rug; amazingly, the wafer-thin porcelain simply nestles where it drops, unharmed.

He's peering down at it, muttering, that intent look on his face again.

"What am I keeping this sentimental stuff for? Nostalgia! I told you!"

I bend and pick up the cup. I ask whether I should put it back in its place, and he nods and grunts. But I don't know why I can't say what I really came for. It'll soon be too late.

"Take my advice. Have as little as possible to do with neighbours and relatives. It's the only way to get any peace. And don't visit retired colleagues!"

It's only half-past four but the sun's going already, and his low fire is popping and flickering in the grate. He sinks lifelessly into his chair again. The morsels of wisdom seem used up. It's as if I'm not even there. I can see he's had enough.

I get in my car and drive home. Moira will be waiting for me, but she's going to be disappointed. We first met when she sometimes came to the office to visit her uncle, because of his refusal to be visited at home. Then, she was the typical gawky schoolgirl, and we struck up what I supposed you'd call a bantering acquaintance. Half-child though she still was, I knew she fancied me.

A lot has happened since then, but now we're together as if in some predestined way. Moira had no idea where her uncle was living till I remembered what he'd told me about this seaside place. Ever since we moved in together, she's been too scared to go to him, to break the old no-visiting rule. She'll be longing to know how it went, but somehow or other, I haven't told him about the two of us. And that was the whole point of the visit.

But I wonder. Did he drop that cup deliberately, having me on a string?

Amor Platonicus

So far as I recall, the term cruising wasn't yet current back then. Anyway Louis didn't go in for it much. If, of a warm evening on the sea-front, an opportunity offered itself, he wouldn't pass it up. But he had more courtly ways of enticing his boys.

He had no objection to friendships with interesting mature men. But boys around fourteen to sixteen were his heart's desire.

The problem was, they grew up so quickly and went their own ways. It was the age-old bind. What Louis craved was a love of purest Platonic essence, a love which never changed.

"O-o-o-oh! My dear Peter! You speak of Platonic love as if it meant merely a marriage of minds!" he would exclaim at a certain stage in the education of each of his successive young protégés. (Let us, at random, call this one Peter. Paul would serve just as well.) The "O-o-o-oh" was a prolonged and passionate exhalation. "That is not at all what Plato meant! Not at all! It may be the received notion, but it is a vulgar and ignorant distortion!"

"Now let me lend you this little book." He rose and stepped over to the bookshelves lining his "library", ran a forefinger along spines, crooked it in a way suggestive of obscure refinements, and extracted a slim, leather-bound volume. The titling was tooled in gold. He had bound the book himself, from a paperback.

"This is a selection from Plato's *Dialogues*. You've heard of Socrates, haven't you? In ancient Athens Socrates conducted these dialogues, and Plato, you see, recorded them. Socrates, of course, was one of the first great teachers. And he knew that for teaching to take place there must be more than a cold, formal relationship between teacher and pupil. They must be friends. Ideally, *more* than friends – *lovers*, one might say. For Socrates, teaching, learning and love were all one, and together led us to a higher world. A world of perfect beauty. That is *amor socraticus.* Or as it has become more widely known, because so it is represented to us by Plato, *amor platonicus.* Platonic love. Oh no, nothing at all to do with love between the sexes." And he added with deliberation: "Or with love *without* sex."

"Peter, you must borrow this little book. Keep it as long as you like, and treasure it. It is a thing of beauty, and, as Keats said, a joy forever. Now, have some more tea."

And then he would serve the Earl Grey tea and read, with lavish expressiveness, two or three carefully chosen sonnets of Shakespeare. They were picked to demonstrate the relentlessness of Time against which there was no remedy but to seize the day.

O, how shall summer's honey breath hold out
Against the wrackful siege of batt'ring days ...?

And to stress the need to be vigilant against the siren-snares of the female sex.

"Isn't that so-o-o beautiful?" he would say, lingering over some Shakespearean felicity. And if his young listener nodded agreement:

"Ah, Peter, *you* understand, you see. Not so many of us do. Don't you think that even now, in the modern world, there could be loving friendships between teacher and pupil such as Socrates envisaged? No, no, I am not Socrates, or Plato, of course. Still, you and I ...?"

I think Louis was the only person I have met who in all seriousness, in the twentieth century, pursued a Platonic ideal in which love, "a world of perfect beauty", and pedagogy coalesced.

As the youth left, perplexedly grasping his little book, the parting shot would be: "Dear Peter, remember this, there are no women in the *Dialogues*, no women. The love of which Plato spoke was always between men."

Yet certainly women didn't find Louis himself, with his charms and talents, unattractive. He was constantly having to ward off some female follower. All his ingenuity was exercised in devising reasons for not being free that evening, or, regrettably, tomorrow. No, would you believe it (examining a page of his diary), not next Tuesday either. Then, if things got to a desperate pass, in a tone of most mournful sincerity:

"Oh dear, it's so hard to explain, but you know I really *can't* get involved in a relationship at the moment. No, really, not at this particular moment. The reasons are – oh! – the reasons are *far* too complicated and painful to go into, but no, I can't even think of it."

It was a perilous act which Louis felt under compulsion to sustain. At that time, remember, it was next to impossible to be "out". He wouldn't, good as he was, have held down a teaching job, might even have had the police thumping on his door. So there was truth in it: the reasons he could not disclose were indeed painful. He would come to me after one of these struggles, white of face and shaking from feelings of deep physical revulsion. His voice would tremble and sometimes a tear drop onto his cheek. I would try to think of something comforting to say. But I couldn't help finding that physical revulsion strangely at odds with what I felt myself. Felt with some urgency, I might say.

Anyway I had my doubts about Louis's glossing of *amor platonicus*. I had read too little to argue and was unschooled in the slipperiness of notions of the real. But I did blurt out to him once that if that was Plato's idea of the real it wasn't really the real world.

"*Do* you know how many times and how meaninglessly you just referred to the 'real'?" he exploded, and heaped me with remonstrations.

Yet somehow we remained good friends in the Platonic sense he affected to disdain. During those years a series of youths fell like wandering stars under his planetary sway and gradually worked themselves out of it again. Each to whom I was introduced gave an impression of being younger than the last, but this no doubt was because I was fast growing up myself. With his unerring eye Louis had spotted the talent of a little toughguy, wiry, volatile, with jet-black hair, from the council flats. "Dear God, where *can* he have got such talent from?" exclaimed Louis with what seemed to me his oddly innocent incongruity of attitudes, at once patrician and democratic. He extravagantly devoted himself to coaching the boy for admission to art school, whence he promptly departed making clear that this was goodbye. Blond Gerald, at fifteen knowingly bi, saw a girlfriend at first once a week as against the several times he saw Louis, but the balance gradually tipped the other way until Louis's turn came round only once a month or so. Then there was James Dean, or at least he was so much the spitting image of James Dean that for a time Louis went through the days like a sleepwalker. But James Dean fell of a sudden overwhelmingly in love with a visiting student his own age and went back to Marseilles with him for a "holiday" of indefinite duration.

It seemed to me fatally predictable, the way each was drawn away by other needs. And each time I would receive either an unexpected call or a wistful note of invitation, handwritten in fastidious italic, to Earl Grey tea. But it was the case of Mickey, for whom the cliché tall, dark and handsome seemed invented, which brought Louis the most inconsolable distress and terrible of dilemmas.

That Louis's horror of the feminine stopped abruptly short of his sister, I never had any doubt. Eleanor was a head-turning blonde of the far from dumb sort. He was proud of her beauty and share of the family talent, the stunning portraits she made in ink or pastel, and cherished her power to attract "useful" people. I knew that they had joined forces to fight the iron Northern will of their father. No son of his was going to be a piddling artist. More to the point, why had he still no place in the school Rugby XV? And another thing, what was all this about Eleanor going to college? What would a girl need that for?

Their mother did not ever *dare* oppose him. But Eleanor had early understood that Louis's secret must never be suspected by such a father. So generous she'd been with her protection and with those boyfriends who were always coming to call for her, with whom she needed her brother as chaperon! When cancer finally unseated the tyrant, the family rescued what little they could from the heavily mortgaged property and came south. None of them wanted any more to do with "home".

Maybe Louis lavished praise on Eleanor a little unwisely to his young boyfriends. For my own part, she was several years older than me, and struck me as goddess-like, obviously unattainable. In any case, she had a formidable-seeming manfriend of a certain age whom she would meet afternoons and accompany on business trips, and who "helped" her while she pursued her artistic projects.

Mickey, though, often slept over with Louis and I suppose spent a lot more time than me at close quarters with her in the house. He was, I think, sixteen; had recently left school and joined some kind of trainee scheme in the retail business. Perhaps not, you might think, quite in Louis's line, but as I have said Louis's feelings about young males were nothing if not democratic. His tallness, together with a certain presence, a lack of youthful frivolousness, could make Mickey seem older than he was. But for Louis this irresistibly complicated the delicious lean figure and boyish features. He instantly detected educable qualities. Over nine months or so he had polished Mickey nicely. Perhaps a life in retail management had begun to look uninviting; certainly, as with so many of Louis's boys, sexual feelings must have stirred of the kind Louis considered, because not natural in himself, unnatural in all men. And Eleanor was always near at hand. So Mickey could stay in Louis's world and have it both ways. Again it was a case, so to speak, of the fatally predictable. Louis stumbled upon them embracing one day in the kitchen.

I was summoned in Louis's still exquisite but obviously troubled italic.

Come as soon as you get out of class this afternoon. My sister has betrayed me. Please don't say you can't.

What he told me, his face white, his voice trembling, did not surprise me. The affair had been under way for some time. But maybe it was inevitable that he had a kind of blind spot about Eleanor. He trusted her. He liked to show her off, and even made use of her powers of attraction. Contradictorily, he excluded her from his view of female predatoriness.

But there was that tense emotional quality in the portrait sketches she'd done of most of Louis's young friends, including myself. I thought I knew very well how to account for it. Especially since what had happened about six months previously.

He'd lent me Dostoevsky's *The Idiot* and promised that when I'd finished it we would have a talk about it. It took me ages, of course, but finally I reached the Conclusion, page six-hundred-and-sixty or whatever it was. I fixed a time to return the book. Clutching it, I rang the doorbell and waited. Then I rang again and waited again. I was pressing the button a third time when the door opened a couple of inches.

"Oh, it's you!" said Eleanor with something like relief in her voice.

"So sorry, I was just having a bath. Louis's not here, but do come in and wait." And the door opened enough for me to squeeze through into the hallway.

"He should have been back by now. He really shouldn't be long."

She was barefoot and swathed in a towel. Her yellow hair piled up on her head left a pale curve of neck without protection and her unmade-up face shone unguardedly.

"Oh dear, *so* sorry I can't talk to you. I must go into my room and get dry. Oh dear, I wish I could ask you in, but I can't very well, can I?"

Well, that seemed obvious enough, and I wondered why she was asking my opinion. She stood hesitating in front of the door of her room, a hand on the knob.

"Oh, how silly. I would so like to ask you in and talk to you while you're waiting for Louis. It's awful of me to leave you alone."

She was pushing the door open and still standing by it hesitantly. Well, if she was having a problem about actually going into that room, the quickest way to solve it seemed to be to go in with her. By now she'd opened the door plenty wide enough and kept it open. There seemed no need for me to say anything, and she made no effort to check my tentative step forward.

"Oh yes, that's sensible after all. Now sit down there" – touching a chair-leg with a glistening bare foot, arched ballet-like – and I'm sure you won't have to wait long."

She rubbed away at herself through the towel, chatting to me as she did so. Gradually the towel slipped lower over her breasts and then swung open. Then she was naked, only a foot or two from the chair in which she had sat me down.

Her body seemed radiant and liquid and I believe I felt as if I had already passed into that Platonic higher world which Louis had so often extolled to me. But I'm pretty sure I decided then that he was wrong about one thing. It was not only attainable through love between men.

I hardly need say that I have often thought about what might have happened if we hadn't heard Louis's car turning into the drive. He was an erratic driver, and usually took more than one go to get in. She had a covering of clothes on in next to no time and was on her way outside to meet him. I could hear her calling:

"Where on earth have you been, dear? T——'s been here ages waiting for you!"

I slipped out and stood in the hall where a dusty light came through the open doorway. Louis came blustering in, a package under each arm, antique vases or something. His face was concentrated with his peculiar look of concern, a look which could make you believe that at that moment he cared for nothing in the world except your own feelings. He apologised complicatedly for keeping me.

I told him not to worry. No, really, it didn't matter at all. I hadn't minded waiting in the least.

But it was harder than ever, over the Earl Grey tea those few months later, to find words of comfort.

Mrs. Permanently

My grandmother died rather unexpectedly. She was walking home with my aunt from dusting pews in the church when suddenly she sat down on a low wall "feeling a bit queer," she said. She was dead by ten o'clock that evening. Sammy asked if she could come to the funeral with me.

Sammy had come down and met Grandma only once. That was in the Easter vacation, after we'd been on the Aldermaston march. It was glittery spring weather and Grandma sat in an old canvas chair and knitted, in a sheltered patch of garden, with her feet on a stool. Occasionally a stirring of breeze fluffed her hair, which had been purest white as long as I could remember. The rows of knitting grew while she and Sammy talked, for what seemed a long time, and before we left she made Sammy a present of an old brooch. I knew the brooch; there was a story about it she'd often told when we were children. Grandfather, overseas in the first war, had been paid a gambling debt; he'd bought the brooch and posted it off; the ship had been sunk on the way, but the parcel was recovered by divers. The brooch was already stained and discoloured. It had never really looked new. All the same, Grandma treasured it.

We stood as the coffin was slow-marched up the aisle of the church, sat through the vicar's commonplaces about some person I hardly recognised as my grandmother, were driven at snail's pace to the cemetery, and watched while the soil rattled into the hole. Sammy wore the brooch.

It was midnight when we got back to find Mrs. Permanently, helpless on the landing outside my room. She gazed at us blankly, with bovine eyes. Her mouth worked continuously, trying to shape some kind of speech. Three doors led off the landing, mine, hers and the bathroom. In that shadowy hollow under the roof, only a faint glow through the sky-light, she was wholly unable to sort out which door was hers. When Sammy asked where her key was, she couldn't get out an answer. A handbag hung limply from one arm, and Sammy had to search through it to find the key. Between us, we shuffled her into her room.

It was my final year at university and I was renting that box at the top of a tall Victorian house of the sort nobody could afford to keep up any more except as flats. Sammy had started coming there regularly. She seldom gave warning, saying she had just "dropped in", and then she'd stay till morning. On summer evenings I would stand at my little window watching out for her as the street below turned silvery and people tortoised along it. If she hadn't shown up when the street-lights flickered palely on, I went downstairs and round the corner to *The Running Horse*. She'd know where I was. Colin might be sitting in the dilapidated "Smoke Room" with something by Thomas Mann open in front of him. He was doing German, was probably going to get a First. He would be rolling a matchstick-thin cigarette from a crumpled packet of Old Holborn, or nursing a pint of cheap Mild. I'd have one too, and go back to find Sammy sitting on the top stair.

She might say: "Mrs. Permanently just went out. I followed her down the stairs in case she didn't make it but she went straight down the middle like a sleepwalker." I might say: "She must know some place stays open later than *The Running Horse*."

My neighbour's name started with P. I could never catch the rest of it, and never saw any mail for her in the communal letter rack. Perhaps she was past even having any funerals to go to, though there must have been a Mr. P. once. It was Sammy who first started calling her Mrs. Permanently Pissed, which soon got shortened. I'd meet her negotiating the stairs with wonderful sedateness, her lips quivering in an effort at "good-afternoon". She was hardly ever to be seen in the mornings. Sometimes I'd hear her key scratching at my door, and I had to go out and put her right. Often she couldn't aim straight for the lock and I had to do it for her. Strangers would bring her home, and stare in surprise when I emerged from the room she had indicated as hers. Once, when I helped her into her own room, she fumbled about for a while and then held up a wizened yellow pear. She kept wafting this token of gratitude towards me, making sob-like noises somewhere in the back of her throat. Some mornings, items of her clothing, oddities of old-fashioned under-garment and whatnot, draped the stairs.

After the exams, Sammy and I fixed up to go to the register office. We told hardly anybody, and invited nobody. It was our affair, we didn't want herds of relations poking around. But we had to have a second witness, one in addition to Colin. Colin had already lent me twenty pounds, making the whole thing possible. The few others we might have asked at the university had packed up for the vacation. Then the three of us seemed to have the same thought at once: Mrs. Permanently was permanently available. We knocked on her door several times and after a while got a dazed response. We weren't quite sure whether she understood what we were asking her to do, but she didn't give any indication of declining.

On the day, funds not running to a taxi, we helped her on to a bus and sat with her bolt upright between Sammy and myself on the seat for three at the back, trying to make some kind of conversation. We only got the back-of-the-throat noises. When we reached our stop, we were a bit early. There was a pub next door to the register office. It wasn't that our indispensable witness purposely headed there; it seemed to set up some kind of gravitational field within which she moved inexorably, and since she was sandwiched between us, we were dragged with her. There was no way to divert her. Halfway through the second dry Martini her eye fixed itself with painstaking care on Grandma's brooch, which was pinned to Sammy's blouse. She made nodding movements with her head. Then she reached out and fingered it. She was concentrating her whole attention on it, still nodding, back-of-the-throat noises coming thick and fast. We couldn't at all make out what it was about and finally distracted her by supplying another drink. One of my borrowed five-pound notes was well broken into before it was time to get her on her feet again.

The official in charge looked distinctly sceptical as he trotted out his homily and then the phrases for us to repeat. Colin, somewhere among the otherwise empty rows of chairs behind us, had to take over with Mrs. Permanently. I expected to hear a crash and a scattering of chairs at any moment. But there wasn't a sound. When I could eventually glance round, she was rigidly upright, her lips slightly pursed, as if she could hold out like that till Kingdom Come – and I believe she could have. Then it was time to pay the fee (I think it was seventeen-and-six in those pre-decimal days), and I fished among the change from the pub for the right money. Somebody had told me you were supposed to include a tip, but I couldn't see why. Presumably the register office staff were paid. Anyway, on principle I never tipped, or perhaps I just couldn't afford it. But I needed some coppers to make up the sixpence. Sammy had a couple in her purse, Colin found one tucked in his Old Holborn packet. Mrs. Permanently looked from her expression as if she were on another planet. But she wasn't, because although her eyes stared blankly in front of her, her skinny fingers strayed inside the old handbag. There was a kind of dull rattling, then the thumb and forefinger emerged with two penny coins wedged between them. I already had one myself and that made the sixpence. Sammy suggested afterwards they were from her "spending a penny" stock, essential in those days for female persons who passed as much time as she did in watering places. I hope she wasn't later taken short without the necessary coinage.

We were ushered over to where the register was spread open, and Sammy signed, and then myself. Then Colin lightly pushed his arm through his charge's, guiding her the few steps forward to the table. Somehow, like a puppet-master, he applied just enough pressure to bring her right hand into the required position. I put the pen into it, and she gripped, and somnolently lowered the nib to touch the paper. Some little arabesques, and there, sure enough, was a capital P, a full stop, a space, another capital P, plainly legible, and a sort of wavy tail, which yes, conceivably could have been "issed". I added the address.

The pub next door was closed when we came out, but as before, our sleepwalker set a course for us. We walked for a few minutes, and then she veered down some basement steps. There was a door at the bottom, a bellpush, and a notice: MONTPELIER CLUB. MEMBERS ONLY. Colin pressed the bell. After some negotiations with a skeletal character wearing a shabby barman's waistcoat and bow-tie, we were allowed in as her guests. The summer afternoon didn't penetrate down here; she seemed at home, among a handful of figures who sat around in the gloom attending to their glasses with a sort of measured deliberation, amid faded plum-coloured upholstery and dirty ornate lampshades. The afternoon wore on and she showed no sign of moving. We left her there.

Next day, Sammy and I were clearing out my room when she suddenly appeared at the open door. She was gesticulating jerkily towards her dress-front. Pinned where it came together below the rather raw skin of her throat, somewhat askew, was a brooch, stained and discoloured, exactly like Sammy's. She was grinning, showing a row of tooth-fillings, and nodding her head furiously.

I had always understood from my grandmother that those brooches with their probably fake hieroglyphic design could only be got from Egypt, where my grandfather had been when he bought it. Of course, Grandma knew little about such things, but was always a good story-teller, and may have made it all up to charm me as a child.

Rose and the Old Codgers

"How's the party? Grossly immoral I see, as usual."

She peered with exaggerated caution into the room.

"Of course!" said Lennie, looking up. "Just look at us all engaged in group sex in every known position."

If he was surprised to see Rose back at last, he didn't show it.

"Right Bacchanalia here!"

In fact, a comprehensive state of torpor appeared to afflict the three in the room.

"Anyway, who wants to be bored by morality?"

"Oh, Lennie, hush. You know that flippancy of yours only gets you into trouble. Actually, you *do* look bored to me."

"Rose, my lovely, if we're bored it's because you've deserted us for so long." Karl had risen and stepped towards her.

"But if you're beautiful, you're not always bright. You should know very well that nobody talks about morality any more. An unuseful concept in a world where all perceptions are shown to be relative. I can't speak for Lennie, of course. I suppose he'd claim a sort of existential morality for the way he lives."

"Well, my darling Karl, I love you very much, but what does it mean, existential morality, all perceptions relative? Just fads, these ideas, aren't they? What about something more concrete, like *showing* you're pleased to see me?"

Karl went over to the doorway and they kissed briefly.

Lennie stared down into his glass. "Oh, we're supposed to be *pleased* to see you, is it? Well, well."

"I didn't mean *you*, of course." Rose tucked an arm through Karl's while she spoke to Lennie. "We don't expect favours from *you*. You're much too busy cultivating stoical indifference. Have I got the phrase right? That's it, isn't it? Stoical indifference?"

"No, no, not indifference, my dear. Stoicism doesn't mean indifference. Lot of misunderstanding about that. But there's no sense getting your knickers in a twist about things that can't be helped. And not doing that actually has to be worked at, you know."

"Really Lennie, worked at? *You*, working at something?"

"Oh, golly, is that Rose! Where *have* you been all this time? Nobody knew *where* you were!" cried Jennifer, half-opening her eyes, which had been closed as if in a doze. Everybody knew she was perfectly awake.

"Heavens, it's Jennifer! Still not quite merged with that excruciating furniture of yours?"

Her feet were tucked up under her full skirt on the biggest armchair. Like everything else in the room, the chair was second-hand, with threadbare patches, dark like sunken cheeks.

"*So* sorry to wake you! But you mean you *noticed* I wasn't here?"

And before Jennifer could parry:

"Lennie, dear, it's been mentioned, you know, that I haven't been here for a while. Thankyou so much for being the only one so kind as to offer me a drink."

"Did I? Must be losing my grip. You're on your feet, Karl, so be a good chap, as my old uncle the Brigadier would have said. I just can't summon up the enthusiasm, myself."

"Not compatible with stoical detachment," breathed Jennifer, letting her eyelids close again.

He elaborately ignored this, rolling *his* eyes in mock-disdain.

"Just stick something in a glass. Anything'll do for Rose, she's not fussy, can't tell the difference."

Is that why she slept with you those couple of times last year? Karl stopped himself speaking the thought which ran through his mind. The four of them knew each other so well, their thing was to say the first frivolous and provocative thing that came into one's head. The more daft the better. But this time he checked himself. He would have both meant it and not meant it.

That was certainly a meaningless thing to say about Rose not being bright. She was the brightest of the lot of them, in many ways, bright enough thank Christ not to take that seriously. She'd got a First when their year had graduated at the new University of Sussex. Then the four of them had just stayed on, hanging around here in Brighton. The place got its hooks into you. None of them had felt tempted by the kind of glitzy jobs most of their fellow-graduates, even those with lousy degrees, had walked into.

Years later, Rose was sometimes amazed to recall how easy drifting had been back then. How you could pick and choose, chuck up a job when you didn't feel like it any more. She wrote about it, for her column in the *Independent*. In the sixties, she wrote, there hadn't been physicists selling beefburgers, double the number of graduates training as solicitors than there were jobs for them. She bolstered the piece formidably, in her usual way, with facts and figures.

One day she read an incoming report about disappearances under military regimes, with Karl's name in it. His letters had petered out years ago; she had never stopped missing him.

That terrible last night they had spent together!

They had stood at the bottom of the slope where the undercliff walk began. It was some sort of stab at a romantic parting. Well, they'd been young.

"I have to, you know," Rose said.

A cold moon hung in the sky; its light shivered over the dark sea towards them.

"I'll have to be nearer my mother now Dad's dead."

There were only she and her sister, who had taken off for some Jesus Saves commune in California.

"And you're set on that crappy job? Jour-na-lism." He syllabled the word unnaturally. "You know, with your talent …."

"Oh, come on. You said it yourself, we can't all bum around in lovely sleazy Brighton forever. Don't know about Lennie. Expect Jennifer will keep him, besotted as she is. I love him too, but not to that extent."

"But she's all right. I mean, now, you and I, we're not fooled by that put-on vagueness, are we?" She loved that way he was smiling at her. "She's tough enough under all that to look after herself and him."

Who's going to look after you, thought Rose. Not me, I suppose,

39

you won't give me the chance. Too bloody proud. All too difficult, anyway, visas and families and culture-difference and all that.

Moonlight eerily on the sweep of white cliffs, and on cold rocks and pebbles, and then patches of shadow. She pulled closer into his warmth. The sun and the land and the life-force, it was in his bones .... No, half-baked sort of ideas. It was just him, she and him.

"You know what the trouble is. It's *you* Lennie wants ...."

"Christ, let's not get on to that again. So I slept with him those times. You *know* how it happened. It's history. There were reasons."

"There always are, for history."

Yes, he should know about that, with his thesis on some obscure point of economic history. And so pointedly named as he was, in addition to an unpronounceable name, by his Marxist parents. For years they had been active in liberation movements, their son born here during a spell of exile. And now, for all his being so adroitly Anglicized, he was heading back to his roots. What was that rubbish he'd talked about morality? As if he wasn't the one with moral imperatives.

She began to laugh, quietly.

"Suppose it'd be no good you taking Lennie with you? No, not much call over there for a specialist in French philosophy. He's reading this bloke Roland Barthes now."

"Well now, white lady, it's not just all jungle you know. He'd find people to talk to."

"But Karl! Beautiful Karl! What about me? What about all that business of choices Lennie goes on about? Can't we choose? Why can't I choose you?"

"Don't know whether the question makes sense, lady. There's choosing and choosing. I'll try to answer in ten years time. Maybe it'll take twenty."

Don't care how long, she thought. Just don't quite forget me, not in twenty, not ever.

They walked up the slope towards the lights of Marine Drive, and on past the Lido and Volks Railway terminus, both shut up now for winter. Their last night.

40

It was telling that stupid story the evening she came back from her father's funeral that had made her sure about her feelings for Karl.

When she had got the glass in her hand, Lennie had beckoned to her.

"Now why don't you risk bringing down this decaying piece of old masonry masquerading as a flat by removing your support from the door-frame, and come and talk to me. Unlike Karl I shall not be so common as to *show* I've missed you. And I can take it, you know – stoicism, you see – if you tell me about the sugar-daddy or whomever you've been dallying with."

"No sugar-daddy."

She turned her face away from him in case of any trace of wetness in her eyes. Karl saw, but he knew. She'd told him on the phone about her father, but she'd said don't tell the others yet. They never talked about such things as "home" and "family".

But Lennie was too sharp to mistake her movement.

"Rose …? Your father …?"

"Yes, I had a little upset the other day. I don't want to talk about it now. But I'll tell you about something that happened just after. I needed to sit down alone and have a drink. I went into a pub. There was this couple of old codgers in there, you know, opening-to-closing-time types."

"Oh I know, the sort that have to be prised off their bar-stools when time's called. They leave a permanent buttock-imprint. Police can check up on them that way, like fingerprints."

"Well, Lennie darling, you speak with the authority of first-hand experience," put in Jennifer wearily.

She had sometimes had to extricate him from bars, and once from the police station. He was no respecter of persons, could be calculatedly awkward. A policeman had phoned late one evening saying would she mind confirming her name and address as Mr. Cottrell had given it as his place of residence.

"My lovely friend Rose will ignore that irrelevant interjection, and proceed."

Jennifer threw an arm over her shins and gripped tight as if she couldn't get her feet far enough under her backside.

"All right. Here were these couple of old codgers, deep in their pints. Then this guy who'd been standing at one end of the bar quietly empties his glass, folds up his paper, and leaves. You know how it is, his skin's not the same colour as anybody else's in the place. And as he goes out, one of the codgers lifts his bushy eyebrows, glares across at the other. 'What's the difference between Batman and a black man?' he says. 'You tell me, then. What's the difference?' says the other. 'Difference is, Batman can go out without Robin.'"

"Rose, do you think you really had to come back? We were having nice intelligent conversation till you walked in," said Jennifer, her eyes momentarily wide open.

"Do feel free to go back to sleep, Jennifer. I haven't finished. Dead silence for about five minutes. The codgers codge away at their pints, you know, that make-it-last-all-day sort of codging. Then all of a sudden codger number two lifts his arm and snaps his fingers. 'Man goes into a porn shop one day to buy a blow-up doll. Sorry sir, says the bloke behind the counter, only black ones left. That's all right, says the man, I'm not racist. Buys it, takes it home, blows it up, and it kicks him in the balls and grabs his wallet.'"

"Oh, Rose such hilarity!" said Lennie. "*Don't* ever take me to these places you live it up in. I don't know that I'd be able to sustain my stoicism. Now excuse me while I puke."

Rose knew Karl was watching her from where he sat beside a battered standard lamp. A little uncertainly, she glanced across at him. Such a rich black where the highlight fell down one side of his face!

It was OK. He was smiling his enormous smile at her.

A Committed Life

Ruth had discovered "the stealing" – she said it as if in inverted commas – bit by bit.

"You know he'd been able to draw twenty pounds a week on his own signature. For small necessities, we've always allowed it. First a couple of pounds disappeared here, a couple there, with nothing to show for them. Well, you can let that go, there may be reasons. But then when you find money systematically being drawn without vouchers …"

"The office staff didn't suspect anything?"

"No .. They knew he wasn't doing any proper work, but didn't feel they could let on."

A deep inhalation from the Gauloise she had just lit up and ash flicked absent-mindedly on her desk. I spread out my hands and was starting to say we'd obviously have to take steps, when she caught one of my hands in hers.

"Wait! You haven't heard anything yet! He'd booked the Albert Hall for a Bob Dylan concert! *The Albert Bloody Hall!* His story was he'd written to him and he'd agreed to do it for us."

She was shifting into her theatrical mode.

"Nothing of the sort, of course. It was all in his head. Now we're landed with having to pay the Albert Hall a bloody whopping cancellation fee!"

I won't name him, our Director of Organization, because it was all hushed up and maybe better that way. In any case, I only remember the whole thing because of Ruth. But such a good thing he'd seemed. We had thought he was really getting down to it, that he was going to get us lots of publicity, not to mention money for campaigning. Too much of a good thing, it turned out. And there was too, in Ruth's words, this "nice student we had *thought* was his young brother".

When Ruth broached the matter with the "nice student", he knew nothing about it all.

"*But*, you see. I suppose he felt the need of some explanation. And it turns out, before he came to us, he was going for this psychiatric treatment …."

"What should I do?" she asked me. "Can we keep it under wraps?"

"Council will have to be told, at least."

It sounded grand, "Council", but of course we were a bunch of nobodies-in-particular. The structure merely lingered on from earlier days, when there were members by the thousands.

She felt for the bottle in a drawer of her desk, poured some Scotch, sampled it, and brushed ash ineffectually from a pile of papers in front of her.

"I will have to give the job up soon, you know."

We'd been over all this before.

"World peace! What can *I* do about it, for Christ's sake? But who the hell would Council put in my place? They just wouldn't know where to turn."

She was particularly good at setting up the dramatic enactment kind of street-demonstration – vigils, dressing-up, face-paint, mock coffins borne along to dramatise the devastations of war, all that kind of thing.

Early in the war, she'd broken off her studies at drama school to work in a munitions factory. She'd often told me about going there from a home with ten servants – "Perhaps, in fact, watching them slave away at my parents' will, a good training for coping, not for evading reality as people believe." I used to think of the factory I passed every day as a child. Lorries driving in through an opening, tinnily over-cheerful music-while-you-work from loudspeakers somewhere inside those cavernous depths, women in overalls and turban-tied headscarves laughing above the noise of machinery.

Afterwards, she always said she regretted having made munitions.

"But you had to do it, didn't you?" I would say to her. For her, at the time, a Jewish girl, nothing less would have done. That was how she always was.

When, some years later, I heard the news of Ruth's death, all I could think of was she and myself sitting in mild air out on the deck of a

Channel ferry. We were on our way to some meeting of international peace groups in Belgium. For Ruth, it was three rare hours of freedom. She had a glass of Scotch in one hand and a smouldering Gauloise in the other. It was one of those soft grey days on the Channel, the sea silky, the sky fanning away into the long distances. Now and then there was a soothing undulation. Part of the railing between us and the water formed a flat iron ledge. For a moment Ruth set her glass down on it. The boat decided on one of its slow tilts. We watched the glass slide along the rail as if in slow motion, take off into space, burst on the deck. The precious liquor puddled out at our feet on those well-weathered planks. We looked at each other. A couple of preliminary coughs. I knew that sign; it was the laugh coming, Ruth's famous laugh. It would begin with a few cough-like sounds, rise to the surface, then bellow out shamelessly.

We both sat and laughed helplessly. Needless to say, heads turned our way.

Then I went and got her another Scotch.

But to get back to "the stealing". Council insisted on the resignation, of course. They also decided to hush up the reasons. Perhaps, after all, that *was* a mistake. For one thing, we were always banging on about the government hushing up skulduggery the public should know about, so how could we hide our own dirty washing? For another, it caused confusion among ourselves. For instance, a week or two later at a meeting of the Campaign Committee.

The meetings, of one or another committee or working-group, were endless, in that back meeting-room in Camden Town. The times I sat there looking out over the sunken back yard at the rear of the terrace behind! Need I say, you mostly felt you were banging your head against that blank brick.

Ruth would be there early, the rest of us drifted in. Harry Upperwood down from Nottingham where he was doing some sort of Sociology Ph.D., thin as a rake like Chaucer's student re-incarnated, a rake upended, his hair shooting forward in stiff prongs above marbly bloodshot eyes. He'd be clutching a tattered sociology paperback and screwed-up agenda papers. Ron Parsons smelling of Devonshire loam and organic turnips, looking as fit as Upperwood did seedy, primed with drawling castigations of Upperwood's "intellectual games", and raring for "direct action" and to "get out on the streets". Never mind that there weren't any streets where he came from. Gemma Brimstone, youth representative, garlanded with melon-pip necklaces and bracelets, spindly white-clad legs emerging from some indefinite white garment, fluttered in like a stray butterfly. Swanston Mathers, of the famous confrontation with Lloyd George, the old school of pacifist, founder-member, sat down good and ready, his papers in a well-seasoned leather briefcase. And late and puffing though he only had to come from Swiss Cottage, Tubby Morrison, hardly taller than little Gemma, his hip-flask winking from the pocket on his vast behind as he waddled to his seat. Not one of them would ever lift a finger in violence (some not even against a blade of grass) or would not later suffer conscience-pangs over present heated words. And heated words there were.

Of those present, only Ruth and I knew the reason for the resignation, and of course we had to keep quiet. Nobody else could understand what was going on. Hadn't he been doing a great job? What had been done to get him to stay on? This led to the usual confrontation about methods of campaigning, "non-violent direct action" or more conventional means of persuasion and protest. Tubby tried his bonhomie. Ruth responded with the famous laugh but even that failed. Ron Parsons had just launched into a diatribe on us needing just that sort of chap who didn't sit around on his backside concocting fancy theories when Ruth slowly got off hers and began casually removing her blouse. I had resorted to gazing absently at the reflection of the windows, curved rectangles of afternoon light, in the water-jug on the table. Suddenly the water gave a lurch as the jug was heaved into the air. Ruth lifted it above her head and slowly began to pour. It ran over her face and on down into a capacious white bra, as if placed there for the purpose. The meeting was adjourned. And as far as I recall that was pretty well the end of the matter.

Except that Ruth had to take on the work as well as her own until somebody else was found. That is, she didn't have to, but she did. It wasn't easy getting good staff for the pittance Council could pay, and they certainly took their time. The fact is, Ruth was desperately overworked.

"Well, who else would do it?" she asked one day when I dropped in at the office to find her down in that gloomy back yard clearing a drain.

"Christ, it's astounding, you know. I'm the only one here who has any idea how to clean shit out of a blocked drain."

Back at her desk, smoke folding itself about her, she made phone calls. There was a deserter sitting downstairs in the reception room. She had to find somewhere for him to go. Suddenly, slapping down the phone after speaking to the C.B.C.O:

"I'm not a benevolent queen, you know!"

As if *I* were to blame for something.

"Another ghastly character arriving at my *home* in the middle of the night with his problems and suitcase."

"And you were up till 5 a.m.? How many times is that lately, Ruth?"

"5 a.m.? 5 a.m. *still* doesn't give me enough time! I just feel he'd get the brush-off with anybody else, whoever they appointed. He came for help and something has to be done."

What could *I* do about it? It was time for me to be off for the job I'd got overseas.

When I finally got back to London on leave three years later, Ruth was in hospital in the Fulham Road. The corridors were a maze, of course, and I had to hunt for her room. A young man, hair drawn back in a tidy ponytail, a ring in one ear, neat blue jeans, came out of a door. He seemed to know me. "Are you looking for Ruth?" – in a low voice. "It's this room here. She's not so bad since the operation. Fantastically brave, of course."

He paused a little awkwardly and then he was off down the corridor. I realized who he was. The "nice student" from before I went away.

Going into the room, I saw, through the big glass pane, rooftops sloping in many directions. Ruth echoed their angles, half-upright on one of those beds that can be partly tilted. The laugh was functioning, but only just. The universe revolved around her. But it was collapsing inwards.

Nobody does her kind of campaigning much nowadays, for peace or anything else. If she were still here I would buy her all the Scotch and Gauloises in the world even though they helped kill her.

Detective Work

I was lying one afternoon on the grass in our backyard, my hand combing through our daft old cat's rolled-over white underside. The grass was brown, and dry cracks zig-zagged across it. I don't know why, at this time of year the camphor laurel tree always seemed to shed bits of twig all over the lawn. I watched Dad pick one up and sniff.

He had just come back from great-aunt Connie's funeral. He looked down at me and said, not really as if talking to me:

"The fragrance of camphor. Linen in chests, heaven knows what family histories."

It seemed to me an odd thing to say, of course. I realize now that it had something to do with that woman who had latched on to him again at the funeral. I say "again" because it had happened before. I say "that woman" because we didn't, then, have the slightest notion who she was.

They were all standing around after the ceremony in the blandly spick-and-span ante-room to the chapel. This time she had a different pair of glasses on, in black frames though just as flamboyant in design as before, and she had dangly black earrings. Yet again, just like before, she asked him what his relationship to Connie was.

He unfolded from his pocket the newspaper cutting Grandma had sent. A couple of weeks after she and Ted had got back home from visiting us, it was headlines in the local freebie, *The Post*:

DETECTIVE ELLEN FINDS LONG LOST SISTER.

She held the scrap of paper under the light and skipped over it. Then she looked up at him through those sensational glasses.

"Well, I'll be damned. I knew Jack and Con all that time but nothin' about all youse. Yeah, I reckon you're sort of dinkum, after all. Sort of one of us. Look – we always have cards Saturday nights. Y'better come over some time."

Did she really say *dinkum*, or did Dad make that up? But cards on a Saturday night! As if Dad could have stuck it!

Yes, detective Ellen, my grandma, had come over here and found her long-lost sister. Connie had stood on the doorstep, her face, so Dad reckoned, as blank as the scoreboard at MCG between matches, though I can't think what he'd know about that, since he never went there. Hated cricket. God knows how he ended up here where, as great-uncle Ralph used to say, sport is king.

Anyway, standing there with no response: "It's me, Con. Your sister Ellen."

To which the answer was: "Don't be stupid, my sister Ellen's in England."

I got the phone first when it rang, like kids do, and heard my grandma's Home Counties telephoning voice. "Oh, it's you, is it dear? Can you tell your Dad we've found Aunt Connie?"

Grandma still had the address in Port Melbourne from which great-aunt Connie used to write. It was some sort of café on the waterfront where she worked. So when Dad was offered the job here and after he and Mum had bought, trust them, the first run-down weatherboard they looked at, Grandma and Ted came over to visit us. They took a tram one sweltering day down to Port Melbourne to try to find the place.

"I bet she used to get chatted up by the sailors down there in Port Melbourne," Dad had said to Grandma before they set off.

"Oh, I expect so, dear, knowing Connie."

The address didn't seem to correspond with anything resembling a café. They crossed Beaconsfield Parade and looked out over the bay. The blue was flecked as usual with coloured sails of yachts and windsurfers and hulking masses of container-ships turned ethereal by distance and heat-haze. The sun was too much for them there in the open, so they recrossed to a cool-looking pub they'd spotted a few doors along, and Ted ordered a slap-up lunch like he always did. When they'd polished it off, he went and asked the barman if he knew anything about the café.

"Jeez, that place! Shut down four or five years ago."

Did he know anybody called Connie who used to work there? This was where a bloke further along the bar, the condensation streaming off the pot in front of him the way it does when the beer is *really* ice-cold, half-rose from his stool, the soles of his feet on the iron struts. He was grinning all over his sun-leathery face. He had already swivelled quizzically to listen to the English accent.

"Connie!" he chimed in. "Everybody round here knew Connie. Moved from here when they shut down. I can tell you how to get there, though. Only ten minutes in a cab."

Well, Connie's blank first reaction on her doorstep in South Melbourne was hardly surprising. After all, as far as she knew, none of us was within thousands of miles of her. There were lots of laughs, tubby little Ted getting his oar in, and they all went inside.

You only had to look at them, even then, when they were in their seventies, to see Aunt Connie and Grandma were sisters. "Spitting image of each other," Dad said. "Chips off the old block."

"Talk the same, don't they?" said Connie's friends when they were introduced to Grandma, for all her little Pommie grace-notes (quite run-of-the-mill back in the Home Counties, Dad said half-confidentially to Connie's friend Hester), and despite Connie's submerged consonants, her bit of twang and gravelliness as if she'd been born here. Underneath, the mannerisms of tone and inflection, the catch-phrases from sixty years before, were the same.

"Is it still there, the Barton Road house?" asked Connie, sitting in our backyard a few days later. Grandma called it the garden. It was summer, the flowering gums tropical red and orange.

"Oh yes," said Ellen. "Just the same, just like it was."

"But the council yard opposite's gone," chipped in Ted. He never liked to be left out. Not that *he* knew the house in those days. He was Grandma's second husband. Odd how she never talked about the first, Dad's dad.

Only Ted out of all of them left, ninety-odd now, in some home, Dad tells me. But it was young Ralph on his spanking Norton 500cc who came courting Connie at the house in Barton Road. It ended up with great-grandfather Forbes putting his foot down, or so the story goes, and them emigrating out here, way back then before even Dad was born. For years she wrote, now and then. But the letters petered out and they lost touch.

Seems Ralph and Connie had drifted apart when they got here, and yes, she had taken up with some sailor who came into the café. His name was Jack, believe it or not. But he wasn't around any more; died some years back, apparently.

"Always been the same, Connie," said Grandma that evening, a bit of a faraway look on her face. "Always just went with the tide."

After a while she and Ted had to be getting back to the Home Counties, of course. So they weren't here when Aunt Connie's eightieth birthday came round, and we were invited over.

By this time, her friends Joe and Hester had taken her under their wing at their place in Mitcham. Way out in the back and beyond, Dad called it, nowhere near as nice as her iron-lacework terrace in South Melbourne.

It was the sort of Oz-suburbia that he said always made him feel like he was on the moon or somewhere. Well, you had to put up with that sort of thing from Dad. As soon as he got more than a few blocks out of the inner city in Melbourne or Sydney, he reckoned he got a sinking feeling in the stomach. If anybody said to him, don't you ever want to see the outback, Ayers Rock for instance, he'd say, all right, I know people who've watched the sun set on it and climbed to the top and found it a transcendental experience, but you'd have to hold a gun to my head to get me to that great pink blancmange out there. Then he'd say, anyway, it's not Ayers Rock, got an Aboriginal name, Uluru, hasn't it? He was hot on land rights; I think he felt uneasy being white and here at all. Which is a bit daft, you can't turn back history. But to get on to Connie's birthday party. We were all there, us and loads of Joe and Hester and Connie's friends we didn't know, all in little knots round the barbecue in the backyard. Slabs of tinnies were being extracted at an impressive rate from an old curved-edged fifties fridge Joe had in his wooden summer-house-thing, which, don't ask me why, he'd nailed a load of old horseshoes all over. The cask-wine was flowing, and we kids were sucking endless lurid-coloured icy-poles, and laying into Hester's Pavlova. All that billowy cream and kiwi-fruit, seems she was famous for it all over the Eastern suburbs.

Which reminds me, there was this nauseating little girl who pinched a bit of mine. About half my size, she was, little as I was then myself, with one of those moany sorts of voices. She already had red and green icy-pole all round her mouth. *Really yuck* she was, I said to Mum and Dad afterwards. Name was Josie. I remembered that all right.

But never mind the kids. Among the oldies, there was that woman. The same woman who turned up again at Aunt Connie's funeral. She was in a luminous blue frock with a pattern in white all over it of what looked like giant man-eating flowers. She had blue-rinsed hair and plastic earrings, and spectacles with blue rims of a design which seemed to have lost its way from a fifties car-bonnet.

She kept coming over and collaring Dad. Couldn't work out who he was. Had known Con for years, *donkeys'* years, she said, but never knew she had a nephew.

"If she said it to me once, she said it half-a-dozen times!" Dad was sounding off about her on the way back home. "Who the hell's she, I'd like to know? Connie's *my aunt*, for Christ's sake. What's *that woman* got to do with her?"

"Well," I had heard her finally pronounce, as if definitively settling the matter, "damn funny things, families!" You can say that again, I remember thinking, kid though I was.

But I could see Dad was ready to blow his top if she said anything again whatever.

She went and sat down on one of the garden chairs and her dress rode up to uncover knees like a Sumo wrestler.

"Josie!" she yelled to the little girl who was pestering me again. "Get over here!"

I was glad of that, at least. And it was how I knew her name was Josie. Yes, damn funny things families all right. Perhaps it's just as well Dad's gone back to the Home Counties himself now that we're sort of related to that woman.

I met Josie again at Uni. Of course, it was some time before we did our own bit of detective work and realized we had that connection through *her* grandma being an old friend of my great-aunt Connie. But I suppose we'd have set up house together sooner or later anyway. So in a roundabout way Dad *is* sort of one of them now, and what's more, I like my old grandma-in-law, as you might call her. But I never heard her say *dinkum*.

Homecoming

Until Grete married my old friend Mike, the evacuation was the only time she had ever left home. Mike met her when he was doing his National Service in Germany, back in the days of our green youth.

It was telling Mike about the evacuation that had seemed to draw them together.

"The booming in the distance had gone on for days. I thought what a funny word it seemed, '*Evakuierung*'. Of course, I didn't really understand. People kept coming in little groups, mostly mothers with children."

They had filled the forecourt and the platform of the little border-town's station. Police and soldiers everywhere, lumpy with guns and kit. It was all very orderly.

Mike explained to her that he had been evacuated too and that in English the word was almost the same.

She told him about arriving in a clunking little train with slatted wooden seats, in first morning light. No woods here, like at home, just occasional stranded trees on undulating farmland which went on the same for miles and miles. A big old house where a rather severe woman showed them the room they were to sleep in. A school, part-time only, too many evacuated children and not enough teachers. Beginning to be able to read newspapers .... The invading enemy armies, the papers said, would soon be "hurled back", and perhaps would never reach them, this long way from the border. Then Grete's little sister Annie died.

"She slept in an old-fashioned cot Frau Stollenberg had. She woke up one morning stiff and hot all over. She couldn't move. The doctor said she needed a kind of medicine which couldn't be got because of the invasion. Supplies of everything were breaking down."

He had been elderly, this doctor, with a white moustache and hands which shook. He came several days running, but it was no good. Annie's hurried burial was not at all like Grandmother's had been back at home. Nobody there except her mother and herself, a priest and a bent old man with a spade.

"It wasn't long after that, I don't know how long, that *Mutti* went off on the little train to try to see my father. A telegram came. He was badly wounded, in some hospital somewhere. She left me with Frau Stollenberg."

Air-raids grew ferocious and a teacher at the school warned Grete that her mother might not be able to return immediately. Then the wireless grew unreliable, with broadcasts fading out, and contradictory information, but somehow news came that the German Generals had signed a surrender.

Soon afterwards a convoy of jeeps and trucks jolted into the town and soldiers in foreign uniforms occupied the town hall. Three of their officers came to live in Frau Stollenberg's best rooms and Grete had to sleep in the attic.

"It must have been getting to be autumn and there was nothing to heat the attic and no fuel for the stove in the back room. That was where Frau Stollenberg lived. And there wasn't much to eat."

Frau Stollenberg looked thin and more severe than ever.

"What am I going to do with you, child?" she said over and over again. "What am I going to do with you, child?" Every few days she went to the town hall to try to find out what to do with Grete. Nobody could tell her.

The same old man who was at Annie's funeral ran messages on a rusty bike. One midday Grete came back from the school and Frau Stollenberg was standing in front of the house with him. He was giving her an envelope.

"That was when I found out that Uncle Johann was living here in our old house. He had Stephan with him. He was asking for me to be sent back to join them."

She had never met this uncle, who had married her mother's sister before Grete was born and taken her to live a long way off in the East. Aunt Stella had become an invalid and died before the war started. She had had no children.

Grete never saw her mother or father again.

For a long time, Grete had hardly given a thought to "home", living with Mike in England.

Then she suddenly got the jitters and cleared off back hardly saying a word to anybody.

At the end of her journey, she climbed down from a new-fangled sort of railbus, humming at the platform. Her uncle held out his arms to her.

"There you are at last child."

He looked older. What else had she expected?

"Put your umbrella up," he said. Outside, the street-lamps hung in washy haloes and Grete felt a sense of *déjà vu* After all, she was repeating an earlier homecoming. Here were the goods yards, in the sodden darkness, overgrown and disused. Everything seemed still and ordinary, not like that day she had left from this same little station with her mother and Annie, or the night she had returned to find a huge man with a beard holding out his arms to her. He had told her not to be frightened of him. It was hard not to be, he looked so much like a giant in her story-books. Every building they passed had bits of roof and wall missing and sometimes a hole right through as if something had gone in the front wall and out at the back. And her own little house with no proper doors or windows, and the walls not white any more.

Grete had lived in the white house on a dirty track leading into the woods ever since she was born. In the woods, red squirrels scuttered away from you and trembling deer peered from occasional clearings. In the town, the important thing was to keep up appearances and not be different. But her uncle, in this Catholic town, went to the tiny Lutheran church down a narrow alleyway.

Grete remembered her grandmother's funeral, people in black, heaped-up flowers, a carriage and horses, and some black motor-cars, at the church of St. Joseph and the Holy Child. Then the house belonged to her father. Every Sunday after Mass they went to the cemetery in the woods and put new flowers on *Oma's* grave. Until the evacuation, that is.

Years later, she took Mike, this young man from the nearby R.A.F. station, to show him one evening where her grandmother was buried.

They suddenly found themselves making love in the woods. She had acquiesced easily, naturally, without thought. It was, perhaps, some way of making up for what had happened between their countries in their childhoods. To Grete, it seemed that everybody from both sides had had terrible experiences in the war.

Only afterwards did her Catholic conscience turn and strike at her, and after a few days she felt obliged to go to the priest at the church of St. Joseph and the Holy Child.

It would be all right, he said, if they were going to get married.

It came as no surprise in the town when the news broke. A foreigner! What could you expect, in the care of a man like that, a Protestant, who couldn't, or wouldn't, speak the local dialect?

She was in her old room again, catching her travel-weary reflection in the heavy-framed mirror which stood in the corner. At that first homecoming, she had pestered her uncle to try to find the mirror. He had dug it out from behind a pile of rubble in the unsafe upstairs rooms. She had stared blankly at herself in the shattered glass.

Now, as she tidied herself perfunctorily in it: "Are you there, Grete?" A push on the unlatched door and her cousin Stephan appeared in the mirror behind her.

And again, with Stephan here beside her, leaning to give her a peck on the forehead, her mind went back to that earlier homecoming. A boy about her own age, standing minutely beside the giant and staring at her. But he hadn't been shy. He began talking straight away, about things like the used bullets he collected, and the soldier's helmet he had found. It was getting dark and Uncle Johann carried a torch. Every time Stephan saw the torchlight gleam on anything, any kind of metallic object, he ran over and scuffed his foot around in the dirt, looking for treasures.

Halfway across Germany on foot the two of them had come, in the last weeks of the war, no transport except for troops, hardly anything to eat or drink. Uncle Johann had foreseen what would happen. He couldn't have lived under that regime, he said. He had found this lone little boy weeping silently in the street one day, and nothing could be traced about him in the chaotic state of things, so he had brought

Stephan with him. But Stephan always insisted that he himself would return one day.

"But you'll never be able to go back to the East!" Grete would say. "Re-unification will never happen!"

It was what everybody said: there would never be *Wiedervereinigung*. Most people in the town assumed Stephan and she really were cousins, and her uncle thought it not worth trying to explain.

There had nearly been a quarrel, that first time she had taken Mike home. He had been daft enough to say that *their* country hadn't really lost the war. "Look at your economic recovery," he said. Grete herself was surprised when Stephan burst out, in that deep man's voice he now had: "What do you mean?" – thumping his fist on his chest – "*We* didn't really lose the war? *You* can go back any time, can't you, to where your parents still are?"

"So, child, you know the house belongs to you now," her uncle said, this second homecoming, as he ushered her in. "Of course, it always did, but it's all in black and white now."

"He's still calling me child!" she said now to Stephan.

It was a pretty special day when Uncle Johann had come home with a piece of glass tied on the handcart he'd made using old bicycle wheels. He even had some putty, in a rag in his pocket. He fixed it in the kitchen and at last they had one room with a proper window. You had to scavenge for everything. If you kept any chickens or rabbits in your backyard, or tried to grow anything, you had to be constantly on guard. Even tiny children, no bigger than Annie had been, took their turns at hoeing or guarding. It was a couple of years before he got enough strong timbers to repair the upstairs floors. But long before that he mixed up some kind of improvised whitewash and Grete helped slap it on the house walls to make them look like they used to.

"What a mess I got in, and him just laughing at me!" she had told Mike.

Her uncle had stood and laughed at her, holding his big round waist with both hands, his great beard frothing up.

Well, yes, she had always thought of it as Uncle Johann's house, but of course it was really hers. After all, it had been her father's and her grandfather's. To think the house was hers! And for four years she and

Mike had struggled in England to save the deposit on a mere shoe-box!

That English phrase Mike had used struck her as comical at first, but she got used to it.

Mike and Grete are a comfortable sort of couple now with grown-up kids. Yes, Grete got over those jitters, of course. And last time I dropped in to see them they told me Stephan, now the wall is down, has gone back to the East after all, to set up a new office there for his firm.

"By the way," he had said that evening, as he turned to go, "there was something in the post for you. Only just come, so I didn't send it on."

The envelope, with that stamp with President Lübke on it which she only saw now when her uncle wrote, was propped beside her bed. Who could possibly be writing to her *here*? But inside – well, only one kind of card has black edges like that. "With deep sadness you are informed of the decease of Frau Magdalene Stollenberg." *Born, died, the funeral will take place, etc.*

It was the first time she had ever heard of Frau Stollenberg since the day she went off from that place in the little train. Of course, Frau Stollenberg had already been a war-widow. When she died, had somebody simply gone through her things turning up old addresses to send funeral notices?

It struck Grete, Frau Stollenberg was being buried in that same graveyard where Annie was. Should she go, and try to find Annie's grave?

She opened a window and listened to the dark watery voices of the woods. Of course, it was a long way, and Annie's grave might not even be marked.

She turned back into the room and tried squatting down in front of the mirror to be nearer to where Annie and she, side by side, had long ago reached up, pulling faces at themselves, giggling. Then she stared again at the black-edged card. The harder she looked at it, the more she felt that it was not there she had to go, not back into that past.

She ran downstairs to the kitchen. Her uncle was frying potatoes on the stove and Stephan was poring over a newspaper, at the table by that first window Uncle Johann had repaired, the blind pulled over it now. They looked at her in surprise as she dashed into the room and burst out:

"Well, I must be off back again in just a few days so that Mike and I can buy our shoe-box."

She says it sounded even sillier in German.

Tupley's Continental Tour

In Tupley's brand of religion, you are always willing, lend a hand whenever you can, make the most of such harmless pleasures as come your way, but look for no rewards in this world.

I got to know Tupley on visits to the home in which my aunt, half-paralyzed from a stroke, had been vegetating for years. You know how it is, I didn't go to see her too often and it was on my conscience. For my part, though, I've always been sceptical about rewards which might or might not be coming up in some other world than this. Besides, conversation with my aunt, in the condition she was, would run out disconcertingly soon.

But Tupley now, you could talk to him all day. I'd often drop in for a chat with him, in his clean bright room with its glossy paintwork.

He was always cheerful, the life and soul of the place. He played cribbage with "the old lady upstairs". Well, she was at least a dozen years older than him, 101 or thereabouts. If I arrived while a meal was being served I'd watch how heartily he tucked in. True, his deafness meant you sometimes had to repeat what you said to him. His eyesight was growing not so good either, and he had spells of dizziness. But he went for an hour's walk every day, rain or shine, and still got along to the Studley Road United Reformed Church every Sunday. One day I found him a bit disappointed at having to give up the last of his voluntary duties there. He had always done them, from years back, when it had been the *Congregational*.

I especially liked to set him off about what he always called his "continental tour". You had to make sure his deaf-aid was switched on first. And all that in the news when it was the fiftieth anniversary of the end of the war got him going about it all over again.

Of course, Tupley hadn't done any of those much-commemorated things like holding the Battle-of-Britain skies against the Luftwaffe, or storming across North Africa in pursuit of Rommel's tanks, or landing on the Normandy beaches. And it was only in the final months of the war that his "tour" took place.

"Have you ever been back to any of those places?" I asked him.

"Oh no, never been back since!" he said. It was his first and his last visit to the continent.

I can see him as he must have looked then, a squat little man of thirty-seven in a drab blue uniform, standing at the rail, the ship rocking gently, off Ostend.

"9 a.m. on 25th March 1945." He could still give precise details. "Yes, that was the date, seeing foreign shores for the first time in my life."

Plenty of time, before the tide would turn and the hard could be approached, to gaze out over level water at the wrecked docks. Skeletal superstructures of sunk ships reached forlornly upwards out of the water, surrounded by markers.

"Never have believed it if I hadn't seen it, you know. All that damage. First from our own fire, then from the enemy trying to repulse us." His memories were punctuated with the clichés of war reportage. "Hardly a building left. Wharves blasted almost to smithereens."

*

"I'll tell you what struck me, during my continental tour. How officers were like anyone else really. Just muddled through, as often as not. It wasn't till I got over there that I really came to see it."

Not, as far as I could see, that it had ever occurred to him to question their being set above him to make the rules and give the orders.

"You never knew what to expect from them next."

Such as suddenly elevating him to the job of official driver. The landings in France had taken place months before and nobody in the R.A.F. Signals Unit to which Tupley was attached expected any longer to be sent over. But one day brand-new Chevrolet trucks were delivered, out of the blue. The unit had too few drivers. Stand forward any man who can drive, bawled Sergeant Dummit next morning on parade. He had never driven anything except an Austin Seven, but the order was "any man who can drive", so Tupley thought he had better show willing. Quick run-over by Dummit of the driving panel, watch here, this is how much choke you usually need from cold, now start it yourself. Once round the perimeter road of the depot, out through the gates, up one street of the housing estate opposite and down the next. Test passed.

"So there I was, a couple of days later, at the wheel of this lovely shiny new Chev. truck, with a trailer behind, and a stack of priceless signals equipment on it. And where were we going? Over to the continent, of course. They didn't tell us that till I'd already been landed with the job."

Loading the truck onto LSTs at Tilbury was a real palaver. The trailers were towed over the drawbridge and hump into the hold, and Tupley thought that was it. But on running in, he was directed to pull over to one side, and ordered to get out of the cab and detach the trailer. What the blankety-blank was going on? Well, guess what? The trailer had to be *manhandled out again* over the hump and drawbridge and onto the hard! Surely the trailers weren't being left behind? There was nothing for it but to wait till the Embarkation Officer gave orders what to do next. And it turned out the thing had to be swivelled round and, half a dozen men heaving away at it, *backed* in again.

"Well, you had to suppose that officer knew what he was doing. You did as you were told, nobody explained."

Just as nobody had warned him about the effect of a trailer behind. These continuous jolts, like someone banging hard on the back of your seat. He had found that out for himself, as soon as they started out. And at convoy speed you're in second gear most of the time, so the North Circular was a painful crawl before stopping overnight at Northolt. Here they were paraded in front of the Pay Officer.

"Gave us a bit of a lecture about foreign currency. Then we were paid in Belgium Francs." *Belgium*, he always said: *Belgium this, Belgium that*. "Funny sort of coins and notes. I made up my mind I'd try to take some home to show Maggie when this was all over."

Each airman was issued with 1 Rubber Lifebelt, 1 Spew Bag, a quota of free cigarettes, and a ration card for the N.A.A.F.I.

*

We'd been talking about my aunt one day, how old she was, where she'd been born. It didn't seem out of place to ask:

"Where did *you* grow up then, Mr. Tupley?"

"Somers Town. Off Eversholt Street. Not much more than a slum in those days."

It must have been, I suppose, at about the time Sickert was working round there, making potent images out of those ordinary streets and lives.

"Tom and Albert both died of T.B. They were my elder brothers. Everybody said I'd get it too. Never did, though."

His father had a tiny barber's shop, with a red-and-white pole diagonally outside. If it was like the places I remember, all you got was a shave or a short-back-and-sides, and perhaps a small packet of rubber product passed over in a downturned hand. Young Tupley learned the rudiments of hairdressing just by being around, and later got a diploma. But the business wouldn't support an assistant, and when he left school at 13 he looked round for a job. Seems there were piano factories in that area, and he was taken on as dogsbody in one. He was taught piano-tuning, and he branched out on his own to make a living that way until joining up in 1939. Of course, there wasn't much call for piano-tuners in the forces.

"I put down for hairdressing. They said there were already enough barbers."

So he was assigned to General Duties, and spent the war on the Home Front running around after higher ranks. That meant nearly everybody.

*

When you came to think about it, once engines were running, ready to pull out over the hump again and up the slope, obviously there wouldn't be room on the hard to turn round a vehicle and trailer hitched together, and backing either in or out with that trailer would be a nightmare. This way, it was facing the exit ready to be run off quickly. Exhaust-fumes building up ferociously down there, couldn't get the Chev. out and into the fresh air soon enough. First thing that happened was you lost most of your free-issue cigarettes, cadged by the Belgium dockworkers. They swarmed around with their funny broken English, and the strangest thing, all in wooden clogs. Next, your first crack at driving on the right-hand side of the road. Out of Ostend, just behind the dunes along the coast; in convoy it was easy, after all. Just follow-my-leader, you didn't have to worry much about other traffic. Pulling up at this big building, must be the Transit Centre, didn't look too promising, hardly any panes of glass left. High up on its front, in large letter, *Institut G. Born*, whatever that might have been before the war.

To one side, a tram track, not running down the middle of the road like in Camden High Street, but on its own rough roadway.

"I heard a tram sound its horn. The old wind-blown type, two different notes. I picked them out as high C and G. It had ten coaches, more like a train than a tram. Current was from an overhead cable. They kept us waiting here at Wenduyne for nine days. Couldn't have been in too much hurry for that equipment, after all, or maybe we couldn't get through. Nobody told us. We were only the drivers, weren't we?"

So this, in Blankeberge where he'd gone with some other blokes on the tram, was what a casino looked like, this gorgeous place standing very high, all made of glass and green tiles. All his life, Tupley never set eyes on another casino. Mind you, here and in Ostend, the sea-fronts were still as the Germans left them, buildings barricaded, big black skulls-and-crossbones painted on them, with written underneath, **Minen.** You kept well clear, but what smashing resorts these would have been pre-war! Cafés everywhere in the narrow streets. Enormous number. Amazing. No food though, the country still very short.

"The only sales they had were for beers, Hock, Cognac and other drinks."

After the war, Tupley spent years building up his own business, a small hairdressing and confectionary shop. To this day, he mentions ruefully that dearth of sales.

"Nice chip suppers for Service Personnel at the Belgium Red Cross Canteen. Nice young ladies serving, spoke a fair bit of English."

*

Brussels at last, April the 3rd. The whole unit issued with a pass. Tupley astonished to find the black-out restrictions almost nil. They'd been still as strict as ever back home. And you could buy almost anything you wanted, like ladies silk undies and perfumes, if only you had the cash, in shops so smart they made you wonder whether it really was wartime or not. And the luxurious Forces Clubs! If only Maggie could have seen those dance floors!

"It was our hobby, you know, the wife and myself, ballroom dancing. Oh yes, we always went, right up almost till she passed away, at least once a week. But in Brussels, then, the noisy scenes spoilt it a bit, far too many of all ranks the worse for drink!"

At the Studley Road Congregational – well, hundred per-cent teetotalism wasn't quite the rule, but you know, a sherry or two at Christmas perhaps, not much more than that.

"But then, you could understand it, there *was* still a war on."

Which there was no doubting when Tupley returned to camp. What he found – nobody had prepared him, of course – was his Chev. stripped of its hood and a twin Browning machine-gun fixed in position.

Next day, the road got worse and worse the further Brussels was left behind. Often impossible to travel at over five-miles-an-hour, sitting up as straight as you could to minimise that banging of the seat in your back, and by 9.15 p.m., when the convoy was brought to a halt, Tupley was exhausted. By this time it was nearly dark, with no moon or stars. But they'd got so behind, the route-forms showing still thirty miles to go to reach the night stop, that the order came to start off again.

Anyway, with all lights on, they seemed to have been getting along all right for about half-an-hour. Then, suddenly, no warning, there was the sickening whine everybody knew only too well. A plane diving to attack. It was coming straight for them.

It hurled along the length of the convoy, only a few feet above, its cannons clattering, clattering, a trail of flashes, a miniature firework display, leaping from one end to another, all in less than a minute. In the pitch-black sky, there was no way it could have been seen coming. Nor could it have been heard above the engines of the trucks.

Tupley fumbled to switch off his lights. It took twice as long as usual, everybody going for cover, spread out as much as possible. Tupley rolled under his trailer. It was loaded with a *Tangee*, a big electric power unit of solid steel and iron: a lot safer here than in the ditch.

"Could hear the Jerry still hovering around overhead, trying to spot us. Pilot can't have had parachute flares to drop. Find us easily with those. Showed Jerry must have been running short of stuff, anyway."

Orders before leaving had been that if attacked from the air all except gunners were to dive into the ditches or any other available cover. This was so sudden that no-one had a chance to do anything. But for some reason the aim of the Jerry gunner was slightly at fault. His bullets went bouncing along off the road five or six feet to the right of the whole line of trucks. And after about half-an-hour with no repeat attack, it seemed clear he had given up and gone, and airmen started to venture out on the road.

"Absolutely amazing. Not a single casualty. Must have been our lucky day!"

If the men had had time to move at all, and headed for the ditch as told, many would have been killed out on the road.

Flight-Lieutenant Fidler, the officer commanding the convoy, took the decision to continue without lights. But on those awful roads the vehicle in front threw thick dust all the time back over you. It was really quite impossible to carry on with safety. Fidler got in a confab with the couple of other officers, and they called along Flight-Sergeant Sterne.

"An old hand him, been all over. That was it then, we were going to halt and sleep rough."

Tupley rolled out his palliass on the floor of the Chev. so that he'd be under the twin Browning-gun with the tarpaulin stretched over the top. All he could do was lie and listen to the guard walking up and down, up and down, and at 5 a.m., with the call to rise, he hadn't had a wink.

In the morning light, a farmhouse and a road sign showing the name of a village. *Martlebart*.

"Breakfast was cooked by the flame-throwers, I remember. And then when the trucks were rolling again, we realised we'd had another near miss!"

A sudden terrific climb, winding all the time, a sheer plunge at the side. Imagine that the night before without lights, in that pitch black! Jokes going up and down about not having any trouble dropping off in the night if ....

"I remember feeling better in the sun, though. Lovely scenery, too."

*

11.30 a.m., where was this? Oh, supposed to have been the night stop. Drawing up in the market place, Corporal Hinge coming back down the line with the news that they wouldn't be moving off again till to-morrow. Good. A leafy valley with a river running alongside. Both a long viaduct where the railway went and the road bridge had had direct hits from our bombers, and a temporary bridge had been thrown over. Nothing on sale in the shops, the locals pestering you all the time, wouldn't leave you alone, for cigarettes, tobacco, soap, coffee, tea – anything. They would pay any price you asked. Tupley could still see, in his mind's eye so to speak, this small boy of about eleven or twelve with four or five hundred Francs in his hand, counting them out.

"Still, the people there turned out to be real Christians."

"How was that?"

Well, Tupley and some others strolling up a side-street, children playing, a woman at the door of a house launching into a speech, all in French, of course. Corporal Hinge understood a bit, thank goodness. Seemed she wanted to show them the graves of two R.A.F. men who crashed near there in 1940.

Arm-in-arm with the kids to the cemetery. Nice that, girl about the same age as little Rita, Tupley's own daughter. Same sort of hair, soft brown and fixed back in a kind of wooden slide. Two graves, beautifully cared for, wreaths about four feet high all made in little coloured beads. Amazing. All through the occupation, so the woman told Hinge, fresh flowers were put on the graves every night, only to be taken off the next day by the Germans.

No attempt at blackout again here.

"Made you feel pretty nervous, after that experience the night before. Hope there's no spies around, I said to Corporal Hinge. You know, sending our position back to the Luftwaffe – the way the C.O.'s got us all parked together in the market place. Sitting target, you'd think, wouldn't you?"

Specially with those two cafés in the market place, all lit up, the proprietor and his family in the one on the corner eating their meal at a table, and what's more, for all the shortages, having a good feed of eggs. None for the customers, though, only drinks again.

"Couldn't help staring! Hadn't seen eggs dished up like that at home since Heaven knows!"

*

No spies obviously, because they got out of there all in one piece. Last night before the frontier in empty old French Barracks, at St-Avold. Eerie. Debris dumped anywhere, echoey shells of buildings, looked as if left in a hurry. Old magazines strewn about, in French, or German perhaps, gave up trying to make out which. Some soldier's snaps of his wife or girl, pinned up inside this cupboard. Funny leaving them like that – copped it perhaps? Nothing on down to the waist in this one, crikey! Just tits and a necklace. Nice pointed tits, and something written across.

Germany over there, somebody said, that line of trees in the distance. Don't think he really knew.

Next morning, Flight-Sergeant Ruff of the R.A.F. Regiment and another gunner at the ready with the Browning-gun on the back of Tupley's Chev. Sweltering day, sweating like pigs. Shouting down all the time – mustn't mind the language – for fuckin' Christ's sake, Tupley, can't you keep out of that dust? Coming up in showers, all over them. Well then, Tupley, at least keep your bleedin' eyes open for Jerry steel helmets. Fuckin' gotta have one. Wanted it as a souvenir, you see.

Spotted one as they were manoeuvring through the Dragon's Teeth of the Siegfried Line; road very bad here, truck only travelling at about seven-miles-an-hour, so off the gunner jumped. *Careful now, might be booby-trapped.* Lying down flat with his helmet almost over his eyes, reaching gingerly out with his bayonet on his rifle. Slid the point under the helmet-rim, slowly lifted. *Got it.*

"Against all orders! Really, he was taking his life in his hands. Typical Regiment, known as a hard-man. Anyway, you couldn't say no to a Flight-Sergeant."

Easier going once properly into Germany. Everywhere abandoned enemy transport and tanks lying where they had been pushed off the roadway by our bulldozers. In places, in great swathes, traces still of tank-tracks over broad ploughed fields. Then some steep hills, even using the forward drive or booster gear you were only climbing at about three-miles-an-hour with your engine running fast, a wonder all the vehicles in the convoy made it. Stopping along the edge of a big field divided into allotments, lots of families tending plots, a stream sparkling in the evening sun. Nobody could resist that cool water, hot grimy airmen stripping off and splashing around. Flight-Sergeant Sterne running over, ordering a few men to stand by with rifles and Sten-guns at the ready. There didn't seem much to worry about, the Germans were too preoccupied.

Another field, unloading the trucks, and Fidler insisting they all stayed fully armed, making it heavy work. Fair bit of bad language flying about. Nobody sure exactly how far to the front, or at least nobody saying, but when darkness came you could see a bright glow in the distance.

"Then we just stuck there, for six days. No information, no sign of moving. Mind you, it was all right, almost like a holiday. Yanks there, you see – American sector. You can't imagine how obliging the Yanks were! Turned the families out of a dozen or so cottages for us. And the funny thing was, those people never seemed to mind. Do you know, the lady of the house even came into the billet where I was and scrubbed the floors. Without being asked. I said to Hinge, I suppose they just want to keep on the right side of us. And keep an eye on their own property, he said. And perhaps glad to be out of danger now. But the grub! That was the best thing!"

Tupley's favourite subject.

"We drew our rations from an American Supply Unit at Mainz. That stuff, in wartime, had to be seen to be believed! True, nearly all canned, but ham, eggs, peaches, cream, almost anything you could think of. All pretty well as good as pre-war."

His hairdressing skills were well known about in the unit. With time on the airmen's hands, he quickly came in demand. Sometimes he spent the whole evening till dark cutting hair in the field. Occasionally, in the quiet, you heard the crack of a .22 rifle in the woods nearby, where the officers had gone in the hope of potting at some game or perhaps the foxes which used to bark at night. Hundreds of lily-of-the-valley were breaking into flower on the woodland floor, and in the clear warm evening, high up here in the hills, you could see for miles around in every direction. Everything looked so peaceful that you could hardly believe there was a war on. Yet several times a day the waves of bombers droned overhead, mostly flying very high. The Flying Fortresses were a grand sight passing over in formation. Sometimes the sun would catch them and they looked like balls of fire travelling through the bright blue sky.

I mentioned the raid on Dresden, which must have been – what? – less than an hour's flying time to the east? Tupley didn't seem to know much about it. Nor could he pick the city out on a map. As for Roman Legions and Teutonic tribes, or Holy Roman Emperors and feudal princelings, fighting over those very hills, he really couldn't say. He had had his hands full. He had been detailed to act as batman and waiter in the house where the officers were quartered, and in the time left over, in the evenings, stood busily cutting hair in a field smelling of spring.

*

"And would you believe it, after going all that way, it turned out the convoy wasn't needed any more!"

On the 17th of April a signal came through ordering the Unit to return to Wenduyne. All that for nothing. The allied armies, after that bit of being stalled in the winter, had forged ahead so fast. The equipment was superfluous.

Tupley arranged for the guard to call him at 4 a.m. He must get his own kit packed and ready first, then attend the officers' billet to call them and help them prepare to leave.

With urgency gone, the plan was to take the return journey in easy stages, but needless to say, it didn't work out that way. A nice little list of muddles and mishaps. Metz arrived at three hours late. But the Yanks, you might know it, had requisitioned nothing less than the *Hotel Metropole* for a transit centre.

"What's more, the hotel was still fully staffed! I couldn't have been more astonished! Waited on at table, loads more top-notch American grub. None of those soya sausages and powdered egg and stuff dished up by the R.A.S.C. in the British sector. Never stayed in a place like that in civvy street, I can tell you. Never before or since."

In the evening, this real hot jazz band, the drummer trying his best to bring the ceiling down, and all the doughboys spending cash like water, and a bevy of French women with them, all made-up and amazingly dressed considering how badly the town was smashed up. Then early next morning, just leaving the town, the engine of Tupley's Chev. misfiring, on a steep climb of all things, bend after bend, gradient increasing at every one. Tupley trying to coax the engine, until, at last, a bit of more-or-less flat ground, none too soon. Wouldn't have done to halt the whole convoy on that dangerous hill. Sergeant Dummit belting up on his motor-bike, already had a sharp word himself from the C.O.: "What the bleedin' hell's the matter now, Tupley?" But helped get it fixed in no time when he saw what the trouble was. Every little thing like that is a hold-up, getting all the vehicles stopped and then all started again. Rheims not until 7.30 p.m.

Astonishing smell on entering the main building of the transit centre here. Corporal Hinge and the others notice it too. Strong, pungent, sweet like disinfectant. Well, it turned out the transit centre was also being used for German prisoners and the smell came from the room where the Jerries were bedded down for the night.

"And have I told you about the good old mix-up there on account of the showers being used communally by both transit personnel and German prisoners?"

Yes, Mr. Tupley, you have, about four times. Never mind, you love it.

Of course, shining wet bodies all look much the same, the water sluicing away distinctions of friend and foe. Not only that, but 85 M.S.U. was the only British unit in this area, and at a quick glance the R.A.F. uniforms were not dissimilar in colour to Luftwaffe dress. And not only that either, but some of the Yankee guards couldn't seem to tell a Limey accent from that of a Jerry speaking English. Coming out of the showers Corporal Hinge asked one of them if there was a chance of getting any cigarettes. The unit had been short for days.

"What the hell d'yuh want?" drawled the crew-cut guard. "There'll be Red Cross packages in the morning. Just you fuckin' wait for that."

Well, it took the Corp.'s breath away. Other airmen clustered round to put the Yank straight. It wasn't long, of course, before he got the message and was yelping with laughter, pulling his own cigarette pack from his tunic pocket and dishing out its complete contents.

*

11 o'clock the morning-after-next, in Lille, a sudden loud explosion just ahead of Tupley's truck.

"We all ducked quick. Thought someone must be throwing bombs at the convoy. Some collaborationist saboteur or something."

No, the front tyre of the trailer in front had burst, blowing out a whole shop window alongside ....

"Well, you'd have thought somebody would have planned for this, wouldn't you? Seemed an obvious thing. But you wouldn't credit it, in the whole convoy no spare wheel or tyre to fit a trailer! And the vehicle right on the tram lines, jamming all traffic on one side of the road!"

Nothing else for it, the convoy has to be slowly marshalled past, vehicle by vehicle. Tupley, the next in line, goes first. As he passes the marshaller he's told to look out further on for Sergeant Dummit.

Keeps his eyes skinned, ah, there's the Sarge with an arm held out, directing him through a gateway into an area seems to be some sort of carpark. Oh, looks like a transit camp. Here Dummit orders him to detach his trailer and take off one wheel and make it double quick, everything's being held up out there. Jack it up then, yank that wheel off. OK, chuck it on the back of the Chev. and get back with it to where the other vehicle's waiting. There it is, already jacked up and the wheel removed, ready for this one to be put on.

"So there I was, stranded in Lille with a trailer minus one wheel, while the rest of the convoy moved on. Corporal Hinge had to wait with me. A new tyre and tube were supposed to be sent over from the Motor Transport Local Recovery Unit."

At least there's a nice hot dinner at the transit camp, then they take it in turns to have a hot shower. But the afternoon passes and no breakdown lorry shows up with the tyre and the Corp. begins to be anxious. He goes off muttering, sometimes wonder how we seem to be winning this bloody war, etc., etc., better find the camp office and ask how to get to M.T.L.R.U.

Apparently it's about six miles out of Lille, so he and Tupley set off in search. And this is quite a lark, after all, bowling along in the Chev. for the first time since leaving England with no blinking trailer thumping you in the back all the time. It's about 6 p.m. by the time they find the unit, and they run straight into a couple of choice oaths from the duty airman. "Had half-a-dozen of us scouring the bleeding town for you, all the afternoon!" Well, nobody had told them to look, and nobody had thought of looking, at the transit camp.

"Too late now, corp! Saturday night. Everybody's knocked off and gone to the dance. Have to wait till the morning. Unless you want to do the job yourselves …"

So Tupley and Hinge hump the tyre into the Chev. and get it back to the transit camp. Not too much of a job getting it fitted though Hinge is a bit clueless about this sort of thing. Dummit would have been more use. Inflate it with the air-line operated from the engine. By which time it's 8.30. No point, now, leaving until the next morning.

8 a.m., following the road as instructed by the C.O. before he left the day before. Much easier than driving in convoy. Glad to have Hinge in the cab, though, with his bit of French. All those people out in their best. Of course, it was Sunday, they were off to church. Strange to see them all. Tupley felt a twinge, Sunday morning at the Studley Road Congregational, Sunday the big day of the week for him and Maggie before the war. But what was the Corp. cursing about now? Nice bloke, but doubt if *he* ever goes to church. Oh, the C.O. hasn't thought to leave them a form 658. Need it at the frontier, it shows your authority to be driving that route – and here's guard huts and the barrier coming up ahead now.

But it wasn't a problem, after all. The guards were expecting them, just glanced at the Chev.'s markings and waved them straight through.

By 11.30 the surroundings were looking familiar, and suddenly, it was Wenduyne.

*

Called in next morning by the C.O., Tupley was asked would he care to run a barber-shop on the camp? With units passing through on their way back from all over, plenty of haircutting would be needed. So he went round with the adjutant until they found a room that might do, and had it fitted with a large mirror and the nearest thing the camp could supply to a barber's chair.

"And *then* I got some piano-repairing to do too! That was a how's-your-father, that was!"

Counted as H.Q. staff now, Tupley was sharing a bedroom on the top floor with Reggie Brown, clerk of the Unit. And one night at the end of April, just before they turned in, the wireless reported Hitler had committed suicide.

"It *would* be the very day new stocks were delivered to the Officers' Mess and Sergeants' Mess. A whole month's supply of beers, wines and spirits. You've guessed it, middle of the night, terrific din. Me and Brown both woken up. Shouts, crashes, it even sounded like pistol-shots!"

Well, obviously celebrations were going on. But this was a bit thick, all this row, and no sign of it letting up. Some of the men who had to be up for duty in the morning were calling out of windows. Trying to get the troublemakers to pack it in. Tupley and Brown had a go too, but it was an hour before things began to quieten down at all. Then, first one of the men and then another went down to see what had happened.

"The sight that met your eyes! Had to be seen to be believed!"

In the Officers' and Sergeants' Messes, the only two comfortably furnished rooms in the whole camp, every window smashed. The officers' wireless set used as a target for revolver shooting. The piano upside down on the floor, all its action out, and the heating-stove uprooted and overturned. To finish it off, a foam fire-extinguisher had been turned over the lot.

For two days afterwards, the same officers and sergeants an airman if he got drunk and disorderly would be up in front of for a bollocking, were down and out. "With D.T.s," as Tupley puts it. No wonder, seeing that the whole month's drink supply had been finished off in one night.

As always, of course, it fell to the ordinary airmen to clean up and do makeshift repairs. The officers and sergeants must be nice and comfortable again. Replacement glass was even taken out of other windows in the buildings, and Tupley had the job of putting the piano in order. He tuned it with a crank he made out of a brass lever door-handle, which had been wrenched off somewhere in the uproar. It would never be the same as before, but you could get a tune out of it.

*

V.E. Day. 48 hours off-duty for the whole Unit. Tupley and Brown celebrated at an Ice-Cream Parlour in Ostend. The Special, coffee and vanilla with fruit syrup poured over, and cream ....

"*Exorbitant* prices, 25 francs, over three shillings in English. But we thought, it's victory, this'll only happen once. It was getting dark and all the ships in the docks were flashing their searchlights across the sky and one ship after another blowing the V-sign on its siren, in morse-code."

But V.E. Day hardly over, unrest among the Belgies. Apparently no attempt by the authorities to check it. Families being picked on and thrown out of their houses neck and crop. All the time, low overhead, streams of aircraft taking released prisoners-of-war back to England.

Corporal Hinge was now attached to an officer dealing with the locals and he told Tupley about them drawing up blacklists of collaborators and informers. There was no chance of these people being let off scot free, he said, not when so many had had relatives or neighbours sent off to camps God knows where, never heard of since. Sure enough, in no time punitive squads were arriving at blacklisted houses, forcing a way in if resisted, shaving the women's hair, and throwing out every stick of furniture, usually through a window into the roadway. The furniture was set alight just where it landed, and the squad moved on to the next house on the list, all quite systematic.

On one day alone Tupley counted a dozen bonfires in the streets of Wenduyne. What havoc. Getting positively dangerous too. Sergeant Dummit, for instance, driving along a street in Blankenberge, in the corner of his eye caught sight of a grand piano sailing majestically out of an upper window. It was right above him: he put on a spurt, a terrific crash immediately behind him. Belgies nearly successful in wiping him out where that Jerry gunner failed! What was left of the piano a mournful heap of twisted wire and wood on the paving-stones.

Must turn a blind eye to all this. Orders not to interfere in any way. And the remains of bonfires from the night before still in the streets on the morning of May 15th when the Unit set off in convoy once more, the last lap for home. All the way to Calais worst luck, no shipping space just down the road at Ostend – the longer the journey, the more chances of mishaps. And needless to say, almost straight away, a wireless trailer jammed under a railway bridge. It was freed by letting the air out of the tyres and pulling the trailer back out again. But the only way around the bridge was to retrace part of the route and then make a long detour … easier said than done, since on the narrow road, it was impossible to turn a vehicle with a trailer attached … so it's one after another, release the trailer, turn the Chev. round, manhandle the trailer to face the right direction, then connect up again. Meant they weren't in Calais till 5.15 p.m., the tide was missed, and embarkation couldn't now be until the following evening.

*

"Taken all in all," Tupley tells me, digging into the box of Quality Street I've brought him, "we made a good show of the war, didn't we?"

It was the sort of thing we British do well. When it comes to it, we are always ready to pull together, help each other out of holes, and all that. So he sees it, anyway. He doubts, too, that back home you would have had scenes like those in the Belgium streets. Reggie Brown had agreed with him about that, though Corporal Hinge said he wasn't sure – after all, we hadn't been occupied.

"Wasn't it a bit of a farce, though, getting sent all that way for nothing? And all those cock-ups, weren't they mostly things which ought to have been foreseen?"

His round shiny face, which seems not to lose its colour with age, though the skin takes on a kind of growing transparency, clouds momentarily. No, it had all gone pretty well, he thought. He had logged fourteen hundred miles in his Chev. Of course, he had been glad to get back to the Congregational on Sunday mornings with Margaret and little Rita, by then growing up fast.

"Well," I say. "It's just typical, isn't it, the way your ordinary airmen were always left to clear up the mess!"

"Oh yes, but you see, it was wartime. You were only a nipper … No one was to blame. And after all, I got my continental tour."

Even that last day in Calais, now – even that was a bit of an adventure.

The men had no French money, but by bartering cigarettes, soap, coffee or whatever, they could get almost anything, most of it done in pidgin English or sign language. Then there was the famous clocktower. You could see it from all over the town, a bit like our Big Ben. Only a few months previously, night after night from the cliffs near St.

Margaret's Bay, where he'd been stationed, he had watched Calais being attacked by our bombers. He used to look for this clocktower, whenever the visibility was good enough, on the other side of the Straits of Dover. It was strange to get so near. He had stood for a long time looking up at it.

Then the trailers had to be backed down the hard by a bulldozer, because these were much smaller vessels than the ones on which the Unit travelled out, only about six carefully loaded Chevs. and trailers fitting onto each.

To cap it all, early next morning, as reluctant light revealed vessels in line astern travelling through fog, Tupley was aware of a sudden change of engine-speed and the boat being put into reverse. The leading boat had run aground near St. Margaret's Bay.

But even after that, after changing course and getting into the harbour, there was one more astonishing thing! They had finished all the shunting about of trucks and trailers, and were lined up on the dockside waiting for Customs, when orders came to move straight off!

"Absolutely no Customs inspection, not a sniff or a whisper. And you should have just seen the things some fellows had brought home!"

The Importance of Remembering Differently

Like Ernest Worthing in the play, Ellie was found at one of the larger railways stations in London. Well, not quite like him. It was the same station. Victoria. The Brighton line. But the hand-bag he was discovered in was at the cloak-room. The bag Ellie was in had been left at the back of a shop a few hundred yards down from the station in Vauxhall Bridge Road.

The police had a theory that the mother must have come up to London by train, dumped the baby at the nearest convenient spot near the station, and cleared off home again. When she was about twenty, Ellie went to find the place she'd been left.

"The shop isn't there any more," she explained when she first told me. "But the back entrance was hidden away down a couple of mucky little side streets. *I* think my mother must have been local, and knew her way around."

"Well," I said, "not necessarily. Let's suppose your mother was some young girl, dead scared, up from the country. Wouldn't she look for somewhere well out of sight, somewhere she wouldn't be seen, if she was going to dump a baby?"

I first met Ellie at W's place. What *was* his name? It *began* with a W. Wally, Willy? I think the first, Ellie thinks the second. Always smartly dressed, posh accent, but seeming determined to wallow in the grime. That much I *do* remember. I knew him only vaguely. Ellie, it turned out, didn't know him at all; she'd just gone there with a couple of casual friends. So perhaps it's not surprising that now, after all this time, we remember his name differently.

I'd run into her again a few months later in some coffee-shop. That I remember *very* exactly. There was a middle-aged man sitting just opposite me, with a cigar hanging from his mouth, a real big one such as you hardly ever saw anybody smoking even in those days when people smoked a lot more than now. He looked foreign, German perhaps, in a thick-collared coat, even a bit like a Grosz caricature. The way the aroma of his cigar filled the place was like I'd noticed when I'd been in Germany during my National Service. He was staring down into a little cup of espresso, a folded-up newspaper laid down carefully on the table by his elbow. Suddenly he took the cigar from his mouth and held it in a short-sighted way, lengthways about six inches in front of his face. He studied it carefully for about a minute. Then he slowly moved his hand down towards the ashtray and deposited the cigar there. A pencil of smoke stood directly upright, then wavered and dissolved. He put one finger on his lower lip and removed a grain of tobacco, flicking it towards the ash-tray but missing so that it went on the table, perilously near to his coffee. Then he turned wearily, as if reluctantly, to the newspaper and began unfolding it.

At this point my eyes wandered, and there she was, Ellie looking straight at me.

That, I suppose, is why I remember the man so exactly. It was, as they say, a defining moment for me. And there was something else, which struck me much later.

Ellie beckoned to me, indicating an empty stool at her table.

I went over and we chatted for a few minutes. Then she went quiet, staring absently over at that same man, who was buried in his paper now. I was trying to think of something cool to say about him, like, look at old Krupp over there, where do you suppose he's stashed all his stolen Jewish gold, when she looked very directly back at me.

"That night at W's place," she said. "You were so kind. Hardly touched me. It was what I needed. Just to be with somebody."

Kind? Had I been? I thought I had just been rather daft. Pretty *un*cool, in fact. First, to spend the whole night on the floor in that place, which smelt a bit, to say the least, when I had a perfectly good bed of my own twenty minutes walk away, even if up in the miniscule attic room I was renting. Second, to lie down next to her, without really being invited. True, the way she arranged our coats to cover both of us in that unheated room wasn't exactly telling me to keep off. But then, as she rightly said, to have hardly touched her the whole night!

And in the middle of the night, W telling that story about how he got turned out of his last place for crapping in the sink when he was drunk. What he kept on about was how it wasn't at all *easy*, getting up over the sink to do it.

I'm looking out into the street as I go back over all that, and here's Nathan idling along home from school. Huge thing that he now is, where the hell did he get that build from, and that shock of black hair? You can see a bit of each of us, Ellie and me, in him, but not that build or that hair. Trouble is, like Ernest Worthing, Ellie doesn't actually know *who* she is. Otherwise, perhaps we could trace such things.

Only one set of grandparents, the kids must have felt always a bit different. That is, they call Ellie's adoptive Mum up in Liverpool Gran, but of course they know she isn't really. And giving their mother presents every year on a day supposed to be her birthday though it was just picked on when she was adopted and she'll never know the real date.

A few days after I'd seen her in the coffee place, I got an envelope through the post. Inside was just a plain card. All that was written on it was:

Sunday evening.

I love you.

No signature, no address. It was a bit of a bolt from the blue. I guessed it was her, of course, but I hadn't quite expected *that*. And I didn't know where she was living at that time. We all kept shifting about in those days, bedsits, shared run-down flats – fit to be condemned, some of them.

A week later, another card. At the top it said: *In the shop, 2.30, just found this, I'll have to be quick.* Then, obviously copied out:

To have turned away from everything to one face is to find oneself face to face with everything.

Elizabeth Bowen

Of course. Shop: that was it. That day in the coffee place, for some reason, we'd talked about books, and women novelists, and I'd mentioned Elizabeth Bowen. Then she said she was working in a bookshop, temporarily, though she'd actually trained as a nurse.

Only about twenty-five bookshops in this town, wouldn't take long to find her.

She didn't say why she wasn't nursing. But that was the way we were, all of us who loosely knew each other, drifting around the pubs and coffee bars. It would have been uncool to stick at anything too long. You didn't want to look establishment, or bourgeois, or whatever the jargon was we used.

Well, it took a few days, even with asking around. I kept at it, and when I did find the shop, I checked the times on the door and waited outside when it was closing time. I could see her through the plate glass, coming and going, tidying up books and everything. She looked a bit different, with her near-blonde hair, which usually fell over her shoulders and down her back, screwed neatly up. When she came out, I could see she felt awkward to find me standing there. I started to say, "Those cards. I had to ...", but she cut me off by turning her head quickly aside. A tear was starting in the corner of her eye. She blinked it away.

"Oh!" she said, "The trouble with working in a bookshop is you always want to be reading the books instead of selling them."

Still, she didn't take much persuading to come and have a drink with me, though she kept looking at her watch.

The pub was packed at that time of day and we had to squeeze in opposite some long-in-the-tooth old blokes whose local it obviously was. We couldn't help overhearing one of them say:

"Mine got bigger, see, after the op."

His mates yelped with laughter and jeered at him.

"It *did*. After I'd had the op. and come back home. Why would I fuckin' lie?"

One of his cronies chipped in.

"Our milkman's wife's a Sister at the hospital. I asked him to ask her about it. She said, they have to cut you open, take it all out, untwist it, and then they stick it all back in and patch you up again. Bound to take a bit of time for that to settle down again. But she didn't say bleedin' nothin' about *that* getting *bigger*."

As I said, Ellie was a trained nurse herself, and when she heard this, she collapsed in laughter, burying her head in me to hide it from these characters right next to us. They didn't seem to notice, too preoccupied with the subject of operations and their supposed effects. She leant against me, and seemed happy, and I wanted to buy her another drink. I was working round to asking her to come up to my miniscule attic. Suddenly, she went distant. Had to go, she said, looking at her watch again.

I soon found out what the trouble was. Fishing around town for information about her, it didn't take long. This bloke Peter, it turned out. I knew him a bit, like W, just to chat to – not much about him. Not a bad bloke, though, I had thought. I'd heard him play good blues guitar a couple of times on folk nights in pubs, and you'd meet him in the street handing out Communist Party and CND pamphlets. But the more I discovered about Ellie and him, the more I asked myself why they had ever bothered to get married. That night I'd first been with her at W's place, she told me much later, she and Peter had had one of their set-tos and he'd just locked her out.

I might also have asked myself whether, if you didn't actually know who you were, you wouldn't always be looking for somewhere to belong. But I didn't know about that then, in the pub. She had her adoptive parents, way up in Liverpool. Yet here she was down in Brighton. The Brighton line, you see.

I tried to get her to meet me again but she kept stalling. I couldn't just let it go after those cards. But it was hard to know what to do about it. Then Easter came round and a whole bunch of us went on the CND march. They were still the big ones then, winding on for miles with banners waving and slogans being chanted and the rest of it. I didn't know Ellie and Peter would be going but when we all got together in the field at Aldermaston, there they were. First day we all marched in a block. I got next to Ellie and talked to her as much as I could. That was when she first told me about being found at Victoria station. I thought of the play straight away. I know that sort of stuff may seem pretty artificial, not much to do with anything nowadays, but some of its lines have run in my mind ever since. I'm always astonished by how closely they echo the realities of Ellie's life.

That evening, when we all kipped down in some school hall, she and Peter went off to sleep way over the other side of it from me. Next evening, though, she came and sat on the floor beside me as I was getting my sleeping kit ready. She seemed on her own, Peter nowhere to be seen. This time she didn't try to hide from me that her eyes were wet.

I stopped what I was doing and took her hand. After a minute, wiping her free hand across her eyes, she said:

"It doesn't make everything all right, you know, being married."

I supposed she meant being married was no solution to not knowing who you actually were. That, and maybe other things as well.

So there it was, a kind of reprise, the two of us lying down on the floor beside each other again. At some point in the night, we found ourselves both in the same sleeping bag. There was a bit of touching went on this time, no problem. Despite all those people there round us.

After that, she gave up trying to keep away from me. She made me promise to come to the bookshop at closing time every evening. And that was the beginning of the end of bumming around not doing a lot except going to marches and vigils and protest meetings. We still did all that but it got harder to fit in, and times changed.

Funny how something which happens long afterwards can put old things in a new light. Like when I ran into Matt Chalmers at a conference up in Lancaster.

We had worked together when I had a three-year contract in Hong Kong. We started reminiscing straight away of course, and I mentioned to him the occasion on the quay. Like most English people suddenly transposed to somewhere like that, I couldn't get enough of the sun. Ellie and I and the kids had been on the beach the whole day before. I thought I was taking enough care but I ended up with excruciatingly burnt patches of skin. And next day I'd promised to go to some island with Matt. Ellie was taking the kids to a party. Felt I couldn't let him down, though going out was agony, the sun pounding down on that burnt skin through my thin shirt. I tried to keep in the shade whenever I could, and if we'd been going on one of the regular ferries it would have been all right, because you could wait under cover. But these were special trips being run that day. So there we were out on an open quay waiting for the boat. What's more, because it was some Chinese holiday, half the population of Hong Kong was there too. There were steps down each side where the boats pulled in, and the next boat was supposed to be due on the side exposed to the sun. It was an absolute sun-trap, in fact, down there on those steps, the heat bouncing off the wall of the quay. I just couldn't take it, so Matt said he'd wait in the queue and I could come down when the boat arrived. But more and more people piled up behind – not your orderly sort of *British* queue, you know – and I began to think I'd never be able to push through to where Matt was. Then I noticed one of the motorised sampan things they were using coming in on the side which was not only in the shade but where hardly anybody else was waiting. Matt couldn't see it; halfway down the steps on the side in full sun, the quay itself blocked his view. I *tried* to catch his attention, but there was so much hullabaloo going on, and he was so determinedly on the lookout over the glinting waters of that spectacular, pollution-hazed, ship-crammed harbour. It was no good. There was no way I was going to catch his eye. It may have been stupid, but the only thing I could think of doing was to jump on the boat on the shady side and wait for him to arrive at the other end.

Which I did. And he never came. Never realised what I'd done apparently. When I saw him again he came for me with a face black as thunder.

"What the bloody hell happened to you, then?"

I could see he wasn't going to listen to anything in the way of a reasonable explanation, and it seemed to me our relationship never really became amiable again for the rest of my time there.

And yet he greeted me like an old long-lost pal at that conference. When I mentioned to him the day on the quay, he couldn't remember the slightest thing about it.

"But we got on really well, mate, out there, you and me. Had some good times, didn't we? Christ, you know how we teamed up against old Greenshanks, the old bugger."

A reference to our boss, of course.

The thing had been on my conscience all those years. Yet it had dropped wholly out of his memory.

Odd, that. Just like Ellie never being able to recall Krupp in the coffee shop, however often I tried to jog *her* memory.

Nowadays, of course, adopted children can find out who their birth parents were. Ellie keeps reading cases in the paper. No good for her, the police never traced her mother. She just went straight to the home from which she was adopted. But ever since I've known her, she's always been looking at strangers near the right age, thinking, could that be my mother, could that be my father? My own theory is she came from Worthing. The Brighton line. I've never told anybody except Ellie, it's too crazy.

The point is, Krupp in the coffee-shop was more or less the right age, and no question, there was something about the way he sat, like she does. Even though, as I said, it didn't strike me at the time, the image got indelibly printed on my memory. Him sitting there, her sitting there, in precisely the same postures. And that slightly foreign look she had, definitely a bit Germanic, and something about the eyes, right down to the short-sightedness, now she's about the same age he was then.

He came over here, my theory goes, in thirty-something, on the run from the Nazis. He put up at some cheap hotel in Worthing. There was this teenage girl working there, used to come and make up his room. Of course, the war started, and he was promptly interned as an enemy alien ....

No, not Krupp or any of his ilk at all, even if the chance of my theory being right is one in millions. Just a weary middle-aged man with a big cigar and an expensive coat and a past. Of course, I hadn't read Proust back in those days, far too busy with marches and folk nights and all that other stuff. When I did finally get around to it, and, quite a bit later still, got near the end, I was struck by this bit:

"... we find also that two people with an equal endowment of memory do not remember the same things. One of two men, for instance, will have paid little attention to an action for which the other will long continue to feel great remorse, but will have seized on the other hand upon some random remark which his friend let fall almost without thinking and taken it to be the key to a sympathetic character."

Perhaps, after all, it's just as well to remember differently. Perhaps I'd only imagined Matt Chalmers held the incident on the quay against me. And the last thing I remember consciously intending when I lay down on that grubby floor with Ellie the first time I met her was being kind.

Aunt Penelope

He's not so quick on these stairs as he used to be. He treks down them from his first-floor flat, thinking of the way Steffie and he used to race each other up and down. Both of them would be possessed helplessly by laughter, and she would be shouting in German, scandalising the whole house. All in the past, that, but she's on his mind this morning. Which is because Aunt Penelope's on his mind.

And oddly, opening the door to answer the curt ring on the bell which has summoned him, he receives a kind of ratification of those thoughts. It is in a small brown package which the postman, looming against the light, imperturbable as befits a bringer of news, delivers to him.

But this ratification is still an hour and a half away when, with the first cheep of sparrows, he pulls back the curtain, and thinks of Aunt Penelope.

Even before thinking of Aunt Penelope, he thinks of the sky. That something which is nothing, with no before or after, a void but a void which is always there and is full of things happening, of everything that happens. He thinks of the sky because of the way light is beginning to seep into it. Low above dark rooftops, an incision of unearthly light where the sun rises. This light falling through the window finds a small square of paper on his desk. In full daylight this scrap of paper looks tired and yellowing. Now it appears to glow, a feeble glow, but a glow all the same, with a hint of warmth in it, and it is what makes him think of Aunt Penelope.

He found the slip of paper in a book, a 1932 edition of Edward Thomas's *The South Country* which had originally belonged to Aunt Penelope's first. It was one of the few things his aunt had ever given him, the time he went down to Somerset for the funeral of her third.

Her first, her Ulysses, had sailed for distant parts early in the war, and never returned. She succumbed to other suitors. He must have slipped this chit of paper in as a bookmark, perhaps never finished the book.

The small oblong of old-fashioned business notepaper has a message struck out in the anorexic characters of some archaic Imperial or Remington:

CONSOLIDATED PNEUMATIC TOOL CO LTD.

121 DINES ROAD,
LONDON S.W.6
PHONE: FULHAM 2277
'GRAMS: CAULKING WALGREEN LONDON
9th September 1937

F/ID
Messrs. Westhill Motor Services Ltd.
Hillport.

Dear Sirs,

RE: Your order No. 627

We have pleasure in sending you herewith Test Certificate for the $2\frac{1}{4}$" diameter Hoist called for by the above order, and trust that this will meet requirements.

Yours faithfully,

THE CONSOLIDATED PNEUMATIC TOOL CO. LTD.
Sid Hornby
Merchandise Department
ENC

Why had he preserved a text so arcane, so forgettable, there in the book, to be come across again as he searched the previous day for a passage he wanted? There were two reasons. The first was of no great consequence, an instance of the meaningless lottery of historical coincidence. It was dated exactly one day before he was born. The second was its rareness as a surviving document of the marriage of

Aunt Penelope and Uncle Alfred. But then why *this* had prompted him to hang on to it, he wasn't sure. The aunt and uncle's involvement in his own life had been small. Probably just defiance of the family sniffiness which had deliberately allowed that episode in its history to slip into obscurity.

Aunt Penelope had been a nice-looking girl in a nineteen-twenties sort of mould. You could see that from the pictures his mother used to have of her. The office junior at Westhill Motor Services, she trotted out one day on some errand, picking her way, in her smart little new office shoes, through the oily patches on the concrete floor of the depot. He had known that vast cavern of a building in his childhood; its image had haunted his mind. But this was further back still, when Alfred was doing his apprenticeship with the company. He'd been on his back almost totally immersed beneath some lumbering old Bedford or Leyland, just a boot and a bit of ankle protruding. She'd been looking the other way, thinking about everything except what she was supposed to be doing, as juniors will. Over his feet she went, comprehensively arse-over-head. Yelps, confusion, him scrambling out, a bit of a cut on her hand, smudges of oil on her nice office outfit. When the supervisor arrived, there they were, sitting on the floor, gazing into each other's eyes.

As a child he'd met Uncle Alfred a couple of times – each time in uniform – before he sailed away. There didn't seem to be photos of him. By all accounts he didn't like having his photo taken, and even if there were any they had been conveniently mislaid. The family had thought a bus mechanic not good enough for a daughter of theirs, and this particular one indecently eccentric. Which means almost certainly *he* would have liked Alfred. He was quite unpresentable, so it was alleged. He had grown huge unkempt moustaches and wore his hair unacceptably long. He was said never to have been seen in church and to have refused to join in any kind of family get-together. Well, bully for him. He'd certainly been a reader, which you can't say for every bus mechanic. Worst of all, he'd been – let it be uttered in hushed tones – a militant socialist.

To be honest, there is another reason for Aunt Penelope having crossed his mind, now that he's arranged his early retirement.

Well, what's the point of sticking it out any longer, all these youngsters, Generation X or whatever it is, speaking a different language. That phrase in *The South Country* about "the harmony of man and work", that's what he'd been wanting to pinpoint yesterday. Now it's all babbling newspeak, management strategies, team targets, development plans, job assessment, performance-related pay. These be your gods, O Israel! To hell with it. Six months to go.

There should be just enough from his superannuation and eventually the pension if they go on handing out State pensions much longer. Aunt Penelope is still hanging on at 88 with the five acres in Somerset left her by her third. She has no heir. She might have been prepared to overlook him getting photographed in the papers sitting down near Bertrand Russell in Trafalgar Square in '61. And being arrested in Grosvenor Square in '68. And even going over to Paris and joining in at the barricades, and getting whacked pretty hard by a *flic's* baton. And finding himself on CIA files for joining in vigils outside draft-card burners' trials in Chicago and Philadelphia. And having political arguments with her third, making him apoplectic, perhaps helping bring on that heart attack. That is, she might have been prepared to overlook his likenesses to Alfred, if he had fallen in with her plan. She had called him down to Somerset and put it to him. Would he take over her third's disparate and possibly in parts dodgy business affairs, sort them out, get them on a sound footing, be a credit to her?

"But Daniel, why *not*? Don't you see, we should keep it in the family. Your mother would have been so pleased. You'd be much better off than with what you've been doing all these years."

She had so much wanted it, would never understand. True, in his youth he'd done a course in what would nowadays be called Business Studies if not by some egregious cluster of neologisms. But it was under pressure from the family; he'd known it wasn't for him long before he took his finals. He had made his choices then, gone off to do other things, and wasn't likely to go back on them thirty-odd years later.

What will happen to him in six months' time? He could go over and see Steffie. She wouldn't mind. Like himself she has stayed unattached, and always seems pleased to see him even though it didn't work out all those years ago. They just couldn't *live* together. Another source of alienation between him and Aunt Penelope. She'd look at him, each of those few times he'd been down to Somerset, in a sorrowful way.

"Are you and Steffie really finished for good?"

Affirmative.

"But Daniel, you must get married again. Can't go on like you are. I hear that flat of yours is just a rubbish tip. Nobody else ….?"

Negative.

There couldn't be anybody else after Steffie. *I'm not like you, no second and third for me.*

Would never have met Steffie in the first place anyway if to your and mother's disgust I hadn't gone over to Paris in '68.

She'd been a little acquainted, friends of friends, that sort of thing, with Cohn-Bendit in his German schooldays. So she'd been drawn to Paris too, as one of his cohorts.

But going to see Steffie can only be for a few days. That's how it works with her, the nicest things can happen between them still, as long as it's only for a few days.

He'd never quite been able to work out Aunt Penelope. That she could have fallen, literally head-over-heels, for a man like Alfred, been utterly devoted to him by all accounts, and then seemingly done a volte-face. Come in line with the family and all its uppityness. Married that quite different proposition, her second, the supposedly good catch who ended up going off with her savings. And to cap it all her third, pompous chairman of the local council, who *owned* most of Westhill Motor Services before he sold off his shares and moved to Somerset, who left her her five acres when he had his heart attack.

It seems she'd had some sort of breakdown when the news came her Ulysses was missing. She'd been ill for months. He remembered her lying in a room upstairs at his grandparents' house. He had slipped into the room one day; she lay there palely like a statue, her eyes staring emptily at him so that he couldn't tell whether she saw him or not. And he ran quickly out, almost straight into his grandfather. He stood at the top of the stairs in wartime Home Guard uniform, commanded him never to go into the room again. His severe grey strip of moustache brooked no contradiction.

The light's brightening now and he picks up the scrap of paper.

That date, of course, is today's date. His birthday tomorrow. This time the half-ignored consciousness that yet another year has drained away, the customary vague resignation, has quickened into the resolve about early retirement. All the same, he starts slightly at the postman's ring, unprepared for it.

He tears his way through complex overlappings of sticky tape, and extracts from the brown package a weathered edition of Gilbert White's *Natural History of Selborne*. Mildly antiquarian, published by Routledge in 1895. Tucked inside are two sheets of notepaper.

That on top is written over in large, rounded script you might think almost childish except that one can see it isn't written by a child:

Dear Mr. Bridgeford,

Your aunt wanted me to get this down from the shelf and send it to you. It was right up the top, you should have seen the dust, it's hard for me to keep up with all the dusting, I have to get right up on the stepladder. I hope you won't mind me scribbling this note. She's getting very forgetful these days. She can't get out any more what with all the steps and it's a worry her on her own in this big house at nights. Your cousin Mrs. Stainer comes every few weeks and rings every Thurs midday. I know it's too far for you to come with your work and all but I wanted to let you know I'm a bit worried about her. She's got to imagenining (sorry) imagening things you know. She said somebody had been in the house the other night, she could hear them talking, but what it was she'd left the telly on. She says she sees people outside too but there's nobody there. She said she saw your wife out in the garden the other day, but of course we know she's back in Germany. She doesn't always remember what happened the day before but she keeps talking about her first husband who of course I never knew so I don't know what to say to her about him and about your mother and all sorts of things years ago. Hope you are well, I'm not so bad considering. Wishing you all the best,

Elizabeth Tipton

Elizabeth has been Aunt Penelope's daily help ever since, as far as he can remember, she moved to Somerset. Nobody else would do all that. Must be getting on for seventy herself by now. Aunt Penelope wouldn't be able to stay in that big place, he supposes, without Elizabeth to cook and clean and shop.

He turns to the second sheet of notepaper. It's clear from his aunt's quavering hand that she has difficulty writing at all now:

You know, Daniel, I always remember your birthday because of Alfred. I seem to keep thinking of him these days. I've always remembered him coming home from the depot one day with some bit of paper and saying Thank goodness, that two and a quarter inch hoist test certificate has arrived at last. I expect you don't know what a two and a quarter inch hoist is but remember I used to work there too, so I knew. And he was just saying that which is why I remember it when the telegraph boy knocked on the door and of course it was saying my little sister Dot had been safely delivered of you.

I think of you and Steffie sometimes. What a pity about you and her. So much goes through my mind, just sitting here in the front room looking out at the trees. At least the trees are still there, I can look at them. I can't get out there to the garden any more but I don't want to leave my house all the time I can sit and look at the trees. Elizabeth hangs out nuts and the bluetits come for them. Sometimes I think things have happened and Elizabeth says I must have been dreaming. Anyway Daniel here's one of Uncle Alfred's books which I'd like you to have, I think it's the sort of book you will like. I sometimes think you like a lot of the same things he did. How nice it would be if you could come and see me. I know it's a long way, and what with your work and everything. Your cousin Josie comes sometimes.

Perhaps he should go. Not hard to know why nosey Josie goes. She'll get the house and the five acres, if Aunt Penelope doesn't leave everything to various church organ funds and cats' or dogs' homes. Or to those two frogfaced offspring of her third who already got their share when their father died.

After all, no real excuse any more, in six months time, for not going. Now if he could take Steffie with him he'd go like a shot. Not much chance of that, got her own life over there, and that posh job, head of city archives or something.

He reads Aunt Penelope's note again. And surely now he is imagining things himself. The sheet of notepaper is beginning to glow, just as that other scrap of paper had done in the dawn light. For the first time he can remember since childhood, a warm current is running between his aunt and himself. It is a slight warmth, a feeble glow, but perhaps has in it a faint draught from that blaze which once must have existed in the marriage of Aunt Penelope and Uncle Alfred. Or even, remoter still, from that which ignites suddenly in the void of the sky and makes everything happen.

One Morning in March 1960

One morning in March 1960 she woke very early.

She simply couldn't sleep any more. She wanted to write things down, anything, now that she was conscious, to shape some kind of order out of this mass of consciousness which would not let her sleep. Anything, any kind of order. A diary entry: but she never kept a diary. A poem perhaps. But she had tried those, her efforts were unbearably awful. A letter. To whom? He had gone and his letters had stopped and she didn't know whether the address she had was still any good. He moved about so much. She had tried phone directories but probably he never stayed anywhere long enough to get into one. Very likely he had gone back to England by now though he had said he didn't intend to. She didn't know how to trace anybody in another country. Perhaps she would make enquiries about where one could find English telephone directories. But where to begin? And would there be any point?

She foraged around the room for something to write with and something to write on. She tried to make no noise; it might wake others in the house. Just a shopping list would do, though even as she was looking she knew there was nothing she wanted to put on a shopping list. She went to the window: she thought she remembered leaving a pencil on the sill. Moving aside the curtain, she saw the sky just beginning to pale. A most diffident dawning. A few blue-red stripes showed briefly and disappeared; a distant part of the sky tinted itself an unrelated green. Unnatural light lay over everything without giving it life. She looked straight down below the window. The lawn in its March baldness. A few bare trees becoming dimly visible.

She found the pencil tucked behind the curtain. Among the things on the shelf at the end of her bed was a small pile of exercise books which she had kept there ever since her last day at school in 1955. She tore out a blank page, wrote down "writing paper". She didn't need any, her aunt always kept plenty in the bureau downstairs, but she couldn't think of anything else.

Then the distant sound of a bell. It was from the Marienkonvent way over on the other side of the hill. You couldn't hear that bell except occasionally when it was windless and everything else completely silent. Before, when she had caught it, she had liked the sound. Now it seemed to jar, a note of distress rather than of joyous annunciation. She was cold, so got back into bed. And resting on a book, she wrote:

Darling, why can't every day have a meaning? (It wasn't a letter, what would be the use? It was just that to write as if she were writing to him seemed the only way to get anything down.) Perhaps it has, but I can't see it. I often think, why can't the setting sun at the end of each day mean a promise for tomorrow? And yet there's nothing to expect except another *day*, another day at the office. But I must tell you how a few days ago on the way to the office I saw some tiny leaves coming already in a hedge, and suddenly for a moment everything seemed changed and lit up.

Soon it will be Easter again. Remember the Easter before last? (Could he – she could hardly bear think it – could he, perhaps, have forgotten?) That really was the best time for us, wasn't it? There's never been another time like it, and now there never will be, because I don't even know where you are. Darling, I wrote to you then (I scribbled so, such an urgent note, do you remember?), come today at half-past-six to Sandstrasse, the far end, past where the houses stop. And there you were, with your bag, standing under that little line of birch trees, when I came at twenty to seven, and it was still light enough for me to see you from the other end of Sandstrasse, and I had my bag too, and off we went.

She stopped writing and sat as if frozen with the end of the pencil resting on her underlip.

There was the time in the woods, on that very windy day, when she had lost her comb, or forgotten to put it in her handbag, and her hair had blown all over the place. And *he* had a comb in his inside jacket pocket, a little brown one, which he fished out and said she could use if she wanted. And she thought, how wonderful, she could use *his* comb, his comb that had been through his hair many many times. And she said yes, but before she could take it from him, he was running it himself through the tangle of her hair, so carefully, stopping at the mere hint of a knot, and saying is that hurting, and even if it was she said no because she didn't want him to stop. And then when he'd combed her hair a little away from one side of her forehead, he did stop, and kissed her forehead just in that place, and then he went on, and combed some more, and kissed some more, and she wished it would never stop.

It had started with the little girl. Sometimes on her way to work or on her way home she saw this little girl. An odd, apparently solitary little thing, she would be playing or just hanging about outside that row of run-down cottages in Burgstrasse. One or two of them had still never been properly repaired since the war. After a while she began stopping for a minute or two to speak to the girl, the mother perhaps peeping from the half-open doorway of the house. Sometimes she brought with her some sweets for the child. Obviously the family was not well off. Occasionally as she stopped and spoke, if she was outside, to the little girl, the father, coming from his work, would arrive back at the house at the same time. Then the father and she would exchange a greeting. She asked a couple of other people she knew quite well in Burgstrasse if they could tell her anything about him. She found that he worked as some sort of caretaker or maintenance man, the most menial of assistants, at the Glanzstoff textile factory, a huge place streaming smoke out over the beet fields three kilometres away. He had been, like all the other local men of his age, in the war, and the injuries he had suffered had affected his nerves, disabling him for any but the simplest work. And then there was the day when both parents came out to meet her, and they asked her, could she please attend the little girl's first communion? The girl had said to them, that if her *friend* didn't come, it wouldn't be a proper communion. And another day, she had stopped there and squatted down, her skirt sweeping the street, put her arm round little Emmi, and just at that moment *he* had come round the corner from the Kapellenweg. She looked up hearing his step as he passed, and their eyes met – he was looking so hard, after all – and she never knew why but she smiled at him and he smiled back.

That was what did it. He told her afterwards how he had seen her there squatting with her arm round the little girl. And the way that full skirt, a sort of red colour so dark from a distance it looked black, had fallen over her legs as she squatted and clung to the form of her thighs and haunches. Well, that and everything, he said. The way her arm was round the little girl. The way she looked at the child. Her eyes. Her smile.

Her hair.

She always caught her breath when she went round that corner now. Little Emmi didn't play outside much any more. She was growing up.

Sometimes she went to that place in Sandstrasse and just stood, under the line of birch trees. Sometimes she put on that same skirt specially, though heaven knows it was old and dull enough, sale-price from the Kaufhof in Gladbach, and she could never imagine how it had worked the magic it did. In autumn a gilt-coloured leaf or two would fall in her hair. She imagined him pulling out his comb, and combing the leaves out of her hair.

"Comb", she wrote now with the blunt pencil on the torn-out page of exercise-book. She formed the letters meticulously on the ruled line as she would have done to present a piece of work to an exacting schoolmistress.

Very faintly, the convent bell sounded again. *Any* kind of order would do.

The Old Kodak

"Imagine! Turning up out of the blue like that!" His mother was half-scandalized, half-thrilled.

At fourteen, he had got used to being, to all intents and purposes, fatherless. It always came as a bit of a surprise when people took for granted that like other youngsters he had a father always around. "What's your dad do then, son?" Or one day, somebody in the street when the pedal fell off his bike: "You'd better take that home and get your father to fix it for you."

He felt he wore his fatherlessness like his clothes, or that it was like the colour of his hair.

His mother kept some snapshots in a drawer. There they were, his mother and father, having a good time. A girlish version of his mother, in short skirts and with a telephone-operator hairstyle; his father in an open-necked shirt, blazer and flannels. In the wedding photos he was formally posed in an impeccable suit. His trouser turn-ups rested on his shoes with fractional nicety.

He must have been a young man in those snaps, but he looked – well, sort of ageless. In fact, both of them looked remote and alien, like creatures on another world.

It *was* another world, of course. The Wolseleys, Austin-Healeys, Rileys, Morris Cowleys – ponderous, stately vehicles – half-in and half-out of pictures; the Palm Court Hotel on some sea-front, Cunliffe's Model Dairy, Freeman's Family Cash Stores, in the background like stage sets. The out-of-fashion clothes and hairstyles. You had a connection with all that. But the people could never be touched or talked to. You couldn't go out and walk along that street, or into that shop and buy something.

There were a few pictures with a white blur of baby-wrappings, said to be himself. Then the war came, and there were no more photographs.

Most of them had been taken with this same old folding Kodak, which his mother said his father had left behind at the beginning of the war. It was a 1920s "Autographic" model. It was autographic because you could write with a metal stylus in a little window so that what you wrote came out on the developed print. The camera still took good pictures, only they couldn't very often afford to buy rolls of film for it. Sooner or later, in the opinion of the white-haired man, his shirtsleeves tucked up in elasticated bands, at the photographic shop, that size of film was bound to go out of production.

However hard he scrutinized those old pictures, he could seldom discover in the background anything that looked like what he had heard about the twenties and thirties. No procession of unemployed, no British Union of Fascists marching to a rally. No slim volume of poems by W.H. Auden lying idly in the grass or stuck under his father's arm. His mother and father just seemed to be having a good time. Hadn't he seen a book about those years called *The Long Week-end?* You'd certainly think they were one long outing.

Quite late one evening, the doorbell rang in the cramped flat they lived in. His mother sent him running down the stairs to the outer door, locked at this time of night. A figure waited, outlined against street-lighting on the other side of the glass. When the door was open, the visitor stood indecisively on the step.

"Who is that?" the vaguely familiar voice asked.

He couldn't help giggling at the fact that his own father didn't know him.

When he got back from his paper-round the next morning, there were breakfast things spread over the kitchen table, pushed aside at one corner to make room for one of the old albums from the drawer.

That ancient scrubbed kitchen table was the only table they had and all their meals were eaten off it. But the breakfast was a good bit more lavish than usual, bacon *and* mushrooms *and* toast *and* marmalade. His mother and father were sitting leant forward over the photographs, the hair on the crowns of their bent heads almost mingling.

"Look!" His mother was pointing at a smudge of face behind half-a-dozen others on one of those pre-war outings. "That's Daisy Snelling! Remember?"

His father hummed and sucked in his lips as if making an effort to place here. But he could see that his father remembered her all right.

"And that's Freddie Hurley." They were on the next page and his father was tapping a knuckle on another of the snaps. It was still sharp and bright, this one, a sturdy-looking youth with thick hair sweeping back off his forehead, hands carelessly in his pockets, white shirt part open and chest thrust confidently forward.

His mother had turned her eyes away and was reaching for a piece of cold toast. "Oh ...?" – a rising intonation – "so it is ..." – the intonation falling away again, as if to say, hardly worth bothering with *him*. But he could see his mother remembered him all right.

He could do the paper round because he had a different bike now, not the one the pedal had fallen off. He was under the impression that his father had sent some money for it.

Afterwards, his father took them for a run in his car. To be sitting in one's own father's car, driving about the countryside!

He was twenty-nine before his father ever turned up again. Out of the blue, of course.

He was too adult to giggle on the doorstep now, and anyway his father recognised him immediately. After all, he himself now bore quite a strong resemblance to that ageless young man in the old photographs.

His own little boy's arm hooked itself tightly round his leg during the slightly awkward chat, the cups of tea, in the presence of this stranger. Then he thought of digging out the old Kodak. At least it would make a talking-point. And it could be put to use to commemorate the occasion.

He pulled out the ancient bellows as the others assembled in front of the house. The soft black leather-like material which covered the camera was worn and grazed, with glints of bare metal beneath. The viewfinder unfolded on a sort of hinge, and he looked at the neat little slab it framed. A housefront's mottled brick. A man with a receding hair-line, a young woman in a once more fashionable short skirt, a little boy. Reiterated front railing, a frond of leaf from a kerbside tree.

Another scene was becoming fixed and remote, departing to some other world. But after all, photographs, taken out of drawers, turned to in albums, however frozen and distant, could be kinds of resurrections too.

"Remember the autographic Kodak?" he said, holding it out to show his father.

"Not sure that I do." His father examined it, turning it around in his hands.

"You left it behind, with that other stuff, in the old house. In thirty-nine or forty, I suppose."

"Did I? Could have done, easily enough. It was all a bit of an upheaval, you know, the bombing starting, and me posted overseas. Can't say I particularly remember *that* camera. There was my Agfa, still had it up to a couple of years ago."

The child was beginning to fret. They wheeled him off in his pushchair, this unknown grandfather beside him, to a nearby railway bridge. Hoisted up to the parapet, the little boy liked to wave as the electric trains whirred underneath. One of the train-drivers, framed in the glass square like an eye in the snub face of the train, waved back, and the child burst into delighted laughter.

The visitor smiled but his thoughts seemed elsewhere.

"Wait a moment," he said suddenly, "let's have another look at that Kodak. Yes. Reminds me of the one Freddie Hurley had. He certainly used to have one *like* that. Don't see how it could be the same one though."

"Yes," he said, spreading his hands out on the parapet. "Freddie Hurley. Your mother will remember him. Killed in a raid over Germany, I believe. Went with a girl called Daisy Snelling. Well, that's a long story. Maybe I'll introduce you to her one day."

Then, hurriedly, he glanced at his watch. There was some business appointment, which was what had brought him here. He must rush off.

When the photo in front of the house was developed, it was shown to the little boy's grandmother. These days she had her hair done with a sort of mauve tint and wore tweedy knee-length skirts.

"Of course," she said, taking out her glasses, "he wouldn't have said when he was likely to turn up again." Her son knew she was hoping he might, and that she might be around when he did. "Well, if he does, you can bet your bottom dollar it'll just be out of the blue!"

But she was never to see her ex-husband again. And how tiny she had finally looked, many years later, laid out like a waxwork in the funeral parlour with flowers heaped around her. How almost imperceptibly faint the echo of that vivid, lively young woman in the pre-war photographs! He put an old bag and a couple of boxes of her things into the boot of his car, parked in front of the Nursing Home where she had died, and drove the hundred miles to where he now lived with his family.

They went through the stuff a few days afterwards. There wasn't much to sort out. But the bundle of old papers, most of them rubbish, with a few photographs muddled among them ... himself and his children ... as he looked he had a feeling, a bit like *déjà vu*, that he knew what else he was going to find. There it was, that photograph of Freddie Hurley again. Still sharp and bright. The back of it, though, was damaged, and you could see how it had been torn out of the album and kept separately.

Of course, by now he had long known Daisy Snelling's son. The two of them got on well. But at first it had been odd, discovering a brother – well, a half-brother – when one already had children of one's own. This brother, it seemed, must have been born just about the time his father had turned up and there had been that quite exceptional breakfast and the run in the country in his car.

Springtime May

Who's this coming through the door now?

Oh, it's Mum. What's she coming into my room in the middle of the night for?

Perhaps I was dreaming and called out to her. She always comes if I call, doesn't matter what time of night. It's lovely that she's always there, makes me feel safe, even though they say that I'm not very well a lot of the time. Suppose it must be true, I can't run about as much as Winnie and Cecil do or go to school like them. Of course, when the weather's nice I go outside with Winnie. Sometimes I line up all my dolls on the front steps. I love my dolls. I've got twenty-two! Dad has to step over them when he comes home. Sometimes too, I'm even allowed to go as well when Dad takes Winnie for rides in his pony and trap. That's on days he hasn't got any rounds to do. I feel all right then, I don't feel as if I'm not well.

Was I dreaming? Something funny was happening, but I can't remember what.

"May, what's the matter? Were you dreaming?"

"I think I might have been, Mummy, but I can't remember what."

"Are you all right then, dear? It's the middle of the night. We must try not to wake up Daddy or Winnie and Cecil."

"I know Mummy. I don't want to wake them up. But Mummy, how can you be here? You're dead aren't you?"

"Yes, my little love, you know I'm dead, I have been for many, many years. But I can come whenever you need me. You've got to get strong like Winnie, haven't you? And go to school and grow up a clever girl like her."

"You know I shall never be clever like her. I'm different from Winnie. But Mummy, how long is it you've been dead? It doesn't seem long, it seems like you're still here and it's still just like it was and we live at Hyde Road."

"No dear, that can't be right. We moved from Hyde Road when you were only five. And I didn't die till a long time after that. But it's true I have been dead for a long, long time. In fact, you should be an old woman by now."

"*Yes*, Mummy. That's right, I am. I'm old. And I live in this house all by myself, and they come to put me to bed in the evening and I can't get up till they come for me in the morning. Mummy, have *you* come to get me up? But it's not morning yet, is it? It still seems very dark."

"Hush, dear, hush. Don't get excited. You'll wake up Winnie."

"But Winnie's not here! I can't wake her up, she hasn't slept in my room since we were children. Anyway, I think *she's* dead now too. It's ages since she came here to see me."

"Well anyway, little love, you go back to sleep now, it isn't time to get up yet."

"Can you sing me that song, Mummy? That one that always makes me go back to sleep?"

Sing me that song, Mummy, I can't sleep otherwise. I hardly ever sleep now.

She's not singing ....

Of course not, she's not here. No, how silly, she couldn't have been here at all. There's nobody to sing me to sleep. There hasn't been for a long, long time. Perhaps that's why I don't sleep much any more. Penny says I go to sleep in the day, but I don't think I do.

How many years since Mum died? Must be seventy ... more perhaps, come to think of it. Here lies Christina Hurst. Wife of Walter.

Daughter May, born on March 3 1905 at 16 Hyde Road. On my birth-certificate, that. Winnie said I was so little and underweight I was wrapped in cotton wool and olive oil. Wonder if she made that up? She was only three herself, and she *did* make things up. Anyway, didn't stop me living to be how old I am now. *How* old? March 3, my birthday. Have I had it yet this year? What year is this anyhow?

*

Who's this coming in now?

"Penny! Oh good, you're back!"

Well, it must be morning. I must have gone back to sleep again after all. When Penny or Maureen go on holiday, Social Services send me people I don't know. Horrid. They don't know about me. Don't know how to do me properly. Don't lift me right. Don't get me the right things to eat.

"*Yes*, May love, I'm back aren't I. Now, how are you? Been all right while I've been away? You're looking right as rain."

"Oh yes, I'm as good as a rotten old nut could be. Nothing wrong with me a bit of being young again wouldn't cure. But I ain't going to be, am I, so no good thinking about it!"

Penny's my favourite. I can talk to her. Not like the young ones from Social Services.

"Oh, I got your card from wherever that place was. It's in the other room. I think Maureen put it on the mantelpiece. All those lovely flowers in the picture. Knew I'd like those, didn't you? Looked a lovely place!"

"It was, May. I'll tell you about it in a minute. Just go and take my coat off and get your pads and then we'll get you up."

Where was that place on the card? Don't think I ever heard of it. Ask her when she comes back. Abroad somewhere. She was going to fly I think she said, her and her husband. Harry and I never went abroad. Of course, Harry was abroad when he was in the army, before I met him. Baghdad, wasn't it? Mesopotamia. What they called it when I was at school, don't think that's the proper name now. Used to be ours then, or something, after the first war. Never should have been ours anyway, wrong that, us going and taking over all those places. Dad used to be all for it, the Empire and all that. Most people were then. Lots about it at school. Harry said he was wrong, had an argument with him once. Didn't help, they never got on much, Dad and Harry.

Oh yes, of course, it was Annie told me that, little Annie. Winnie's youngest. Harry and I never had any, so I suppose Annie's my ... what d'you call it? ... next of kin, I suppose. If Winnie's dead now, which she is, I think.

Must ask her again what the proper name is. I *have* heard it, on the wireless. Lots about it a little while ago, another war. Wars, wars, wars! Always one somewhere, all my life.

Just imagine, people now, go all over the place. Go for their holidays, or go and get jobs, like Annie in Canada. Vanwhatd'youcallit. Don't remember we ever went out of Sussex, Harry and me.

I used to think sometimes, perhaps Harry couldn't cope with kids anyway. Dad used to carry on, about time we got on with it and had some, weren't we having any. I tried to keep him off that with Harry.

Yes, of course, Winnie *did* die. It was when Annie was last here, over for the funeral and everything. Think she brought her eldest boy, didn't she, that big one. At university now, I think she told me. Goodness! None of us ever went to university. Only nobs went in those days. Not that Winnie would have minded being a bit of a nob if she'd had the chance. Voting for the blessed Tories all those years, like Dad.

I didn't even go to school till I was eight. Cecil went in the navy, said they taught him all *sorts* of things there. Got drowned, dear oh dear, don't want to think about that. Upset us all so much.

I couldn't go to Winnie's burial, of course. Can't go out now, don't want to. Almost like when I was a little girl again. When they were here that last time Annie's Donald said they would try to get me outside in the garden or take me somewhere in their car, but I said no. Afraid they might drop me getting me down the steps. Or I might get caught short. Can't stop myself now, why I have to have the pads. Donald said he could easily have something put there on the steps so they could wheel me out. Lots of old people have that in Canada he said. Can't always catch what he says, that Canadian way of talking. Still, he's very nice anyway.

Don't want to be buried myself, want to be cremated like Harry. Not as if you're going anywhere afterwards and have to be kept whole, like Winnie thought. Daft of her, that.

*

What's that? Singing? Yes, of course! The children singing again, over the road somewhere in the trees. Funny how they sing like that in the trees. Is it the school lets them out to sing there? All those same songs we used to sing at school. At least, it sounds like the same songs, but I can't quite make them out. Isn't that Youth's the season made for joys? How did it go now … that's it, like that. Lovely to hear them singing like that, somewhere in the trees, with the birds, and the sun on the leaves ….

"Oh Maureen, dear! Are you here already? Is it tea time? I thought I'd only just had lunch."

"Hello, May love, how are you this afternoon? I *think* you might have been asleep. That's why you didn't hear me come in and call."

"No dear, I wasn't asleep. I've been listening to the children singing again over there. Ever so nice, the way they sing in the trees, isn't it?"

"Well, May, I'm afraid I never hear them. They're not singing now are they?"

"No, they're not singing now, they've stopped. But they always stop at tea-time."

"Well dear, I'm sure they're lovely. Now then, shall I get your tea or do you need the commode first?"

There, she doesn't believe me again. Thinks I just hear the children in my sleep. Harry would have heard them if he was still here. All our outings and everything! Our real good rairnts, like he called them. He was right. We only needed the two of us, for everything.

Not when he was away in the war, of course. I had to be an air raid warden then. On my identity card, like we all had to have. Certificate of Official Capacity, or something like that it said, Air Raid Wardens Service. Signed by that Tom Semple, A.R.P. Sub-Controller, I remember. Queer chap, unfit for the army, didn't like him much. Used to try it on with the girls, needless to say, all their fellows away. I had to do fire-watching, nights. Go with the other girls to the canteen and all that. That was all right. I liked one or two of them. Rosie Wilkins. Met her years after, coming out of Debenhams. Was Harry dead already then? Debenhams which before that was Robinsons Haberdashers, where I worked when I left school.

*

"Can you leave that top window open a bit, Maureen love? I feel too hot in here."

"Well, all right, but the girls must close it when they come to put you to bed. Good thing we got those new windows done for you, though."

Since the burglaries. All newfangled sorts of things. I don't like them like the old ones that were always here when Harry was here, the nice old wooden ones. But they're two lots of glass, whatever they call that, and they've got all these complicated locks, they say nobody can get in now. Good thing I don't have to do them, I wouldn't know how.

"Oh yes, I don't want another one of those burglars coming in my room in the night!"

That nasty tall thin man. Don't know why, reminded me of that queer Tom Semple. But couldn't see his face. Didn't want to. I tried to press my alarm button but he snatched it from me and threw it in the corner. Could see I couldn't move though. Good thing, Penny said, left me alone, just grabbed a few things and went. I don't know what he took. Penny and Maureen went through everything afterwards but I couldn't remember properly what things I still had in the house. Perhaps from not being able to get about now I forget what's there and what isn't. What things I've got rid of one way or another. But I *did* think there was still that photo album, nice real leather binding, sort of deep blue, with "Family Album" in that nice gold lettering things used to have. Pictures of Mum and Dad in it, their wedding, and all things like that.

Told Annie. She said she couldn't remember me having *that* photo album ever.

*

Goodness, a man coming through the door again now! Oh dear, dear! Not one of those burglars again!

No, it's not a burglar!

"I know who *you* are, don't I? As if I couldn't!"

"Well, course it's me, who else do you think?"

"Creeping in just the way you always do when you think I'm already asleep. Even though you know I never go to sleep till you come!"

"Not asleep now though, are you?"

"No, I don't think so. Unless it's still the war, is it Harry? When you were away so much. Remember sometimes you used to manage to get down here just for a night, and creep in after midnight, when I really had gone off 'cos I wasn't expecting you?"

"Can't still be the war, can it, you old nincompoop? Finished, didn't it, and I came home."

"*Course* you did. But what about that time you came and I was out fire-watching all night, and then I only just caught you on the path as I was coming back in the morning and you were going out again?"

"Tear or two, wasn't there? And we didn't get *that* much, did we? Glad you're not asleep now though, we can have one of our confabs."

"Oh yes, Harry, our bedtime confabs! Like we always had, all those years, till you went and got ill."

"Got ill? Those doctors did for me. All that poppycock about cancer! What do they know about anything?"

"But it was, though, you know, Harry. I know you would never have it till the day you went off, but it was!"

"Oh well, my bunch of springtime May, no use crying over spilt milk is it?"

"Bunch of springtime May! Gracious, it's a long time since I heard you call me that, Harry! Not much springtime about me now, I reckon!"

"Never mind any of that, May. Far as I'm concerned you were always springtime. Even if it was blowing a gale off the sea and stoking up the white horses or the clouds coming down like a thick overcoat on the downs or the weather-vane in the garden round to nor-east and a black sky and the smell of snow coming. Every time we sat out there in the back under the shelter till it got dark!"

"Our old bus-shelter! That you got cheap when they were replacing them with those horrid concrete things! Is it still there? I haven't been out there for so long."

"Sometimes when I went to lock up I slipped back out there again, didn't I? – to see if I could hear an owl, so I could come in and tell you when you were in bed. Springtime May in bed! And then we could have a confab, couldn't we?"

"I thought that's where you'd been then, Harry, when you just came in. Did you hear old Barney, out there?"

"Old Barney's gone, or died, ain't he. Think he roosted in the old water tower, but could never get near enough to see. We haven't heard him for a while, have we."

"No, of course! Knew that, didn't I?"

"Course you did, you old nincompoop! Anyway, the tawneys sound better, the to-whoers. What I really like to hear, but usually have to go further afield than the garden."

"But think how we used to always go over it all again, wherever we'd been that day. Always did that at bedtime."

"That's it! Might have been wet and we scuffed around getting gumboots on and stodged up the hill and all along the top till the track down past the old school. Primroses out. Pair of wild duck. The sun came out just for a couple of minutes right then and the drake's feathers shone like billy-o. Green woodpeckers in the wood near the railway. Rain came on hard so we had to run for the 17 bus at the crossroads."

"Yes, home to our own fire! Still alight, that way you stacked it up with wet coaldust!"

"Well, got to know the trick of it, haven't you? But could've been one of those fine days. Clearing that *ancient* old stile with your secateurs, remember? *Choked* with brambles. Your idea that, taking secateurs, good idea. A real good rairnt ... and after, a real long sunset. Watching it from the front seat of the bus all the way home."

"What about the old watermill? The stuck iron wheel that was all rusting away. And then the little waterfall that comes down through the woods."

"You *know* when we went to the waterfall. You know what happened there."

"Don't I just, too!" Got to the waterfall and there was that log. Just the job for a sit-down, you said. You always could pick a good log for a sit-down, Harry."

"Well, specially if there was something like a waterfall and a chiff-chaff singing, which there was. You've got to have a sit-down when there's all that."

"So we sat down on the log, and we listened. The water tumbling down, and over the top of the sound of the water, the chiff-chaff in its bush. And you said: 'Hark at that water wish-washing and that chiff-chaff chiff-chaffing away! Isn't that the best sound in the whole world?' And you know what I thought?"

"Well, you told me, after, didn't you."

"I thought, 'He's the one for me!'"

"And I put my arm round you. You didn't mind."

"We listened some more, didn't we."

"Then I said: 'What about it, May?' 'What about what?' you said. 'Us,' I said. 'Us getting married. It's what I want, if you want.' You didn't answer straight away. The water just went on the same but the chiff-chaff flitted and a dunnock came instead."

"But then I said: 'How did you guess, Harry, it was what I wanted?'"

"I didn't guess. I just thought I had to say it, one day. I knew I had to say it, sooner or later. You know what they say, 'Faint heart never won fair lady.'"

"I had to laugh when you said that! I laughed and laughed, louder than the waterfall. Fair lady! Me!"

I think I'm laughing now, here in bed in the dark, just to think of it. Can't stop laughing, shaking all over, if it *is* laughing.

Dad wasn't too pleased. Grumbled. What's *he* ever going to make of himself, he said. But he had to put up with it.

Came straight out with things, Harry, didn't matter who it was. I liked that. Faint heart? No fear!

"Harry? Are you still there Harry? Have you gone out the back again Harry, to listen for old Barney?"

*

Oh dear dear, I'm feeling terrible since Harry came to see me. When was that? How many days ago? He hasn't been since. I've got this ache or whatever it is, I don't know where. Stomach-ache is it? I don't want anything to eat. Penny and Maureen and the girls keep trying to make me have something, bringing me things to eat or drink. Penny said I haven't had anything for three days. I don't know, perhaps she's right.

The girls who put me to bed have just gone, that red-haired one, I think, and the one with the voice I don't like. *Her* all right, I can't bear that voice. Doesn't lift right. Made my ache worse than ever.

I don't know what time it is now, can't see whether it's light or dark. Did Maureen stay later than usual? Wasn't she still here when those girls came?

I tried to smile at her and say something nice, thanks for staying with me, and all that. But couldn't seem to. Don't think I smiled or said anything at all.

Oh, but that's the children singing! Funny, they don't usually sing in the evening. And how can I hear them here in the back room, the bedroom? They're always out at the front.

Have they come round to the back, in the garden? Under the shelter perhaps, Harry's and mine, where we always sat?

Oh anyway, that's good, I feel all right now.

Imperfect Continuous

In 1987 Russell Hanslope came upon his old notebooks of "thoughts". He was turning out years of accumulated papers to see what he could ditch before moving in with Camilla.

He had started writing down these thoughts in 1950, at the age of thirteen. Some were thoughts he found in his reading, and some his own. The writings seemed to have ceased almost exactly ten years later, when he was twenty-three.

He had set down in careful handwriting: "There is such a propensity in mankind toward deceiving and being deceived, that one cannot relate any thing from common report, without expressing some degree of doubt or suspicion."

It was a quotation, apparently, from Gilbert White. He didn't think he could have read White at that age but the words, somewhere, must have caught his attention and taken a hold.

"I believe in the ultimate perfectibility of man." He had written this on the next page of the notebook. It didn't seem to be a quotation. Well, he said to himself, if I wrote that I really was in need of some degree of doubt or suspicion.

"Mustn't I also, then, believe in my own perfectibility as an individual? Otherwise how can the perfectibility of man follow logically?"

Pretty short shrift from Camilla if she reads *this*!

Running through the cluttered filing-cabinet his mind had become, he tried to dredge up another "thought", one which he had only come across long after he had stopped having time to write such things down. Was it Lawrence? Something about there being "no perfection, no consummation, nothing finished." Now, at fifty, he could see that this youthful collection of "thoughts" was a mere thrashing-around.

One Sunday morning in 1951, a year or two before he must have written those words, in the vestry after serving at the altar for 8 a.m. Communion, Russell had asked the vicar whether "he did not think it time to demythologize religion." The Reverend Davies had just hung his cassock on its hook and was about to stow away the chalice in its cupboard. He stopped short, one hand raised with the big old iron key to the cupboard in it. A blustering but kindly Welshman, he had taken young Russell rather under his wing. But Russell could not help being amused when he remembered the look of baffled anxiety which had appeared on the Reverend's face. Perhaps he could not quite put his finger on the approved formula, or perhaps it was an entirely new idea to him. Russell had had to remind him to lock the cupboard door.

No, perfectibility was not what had really been bothering him. It was what followed when you took up the word "demythologize". It was a terrific word, after all. He had come across it in something he had been reading – was it *The Listener* or some such paper? – in the school library. Immediately it had struck home. It was a word you could get your teeth into. It was a word he had been looking for, or waiting for to come his way: it answered exactly to something. All the "beliefs" and as his mother would say "done things" which had jostled his young life more or less ever since he could remember, remonstrated with it, made claims upon it. Just kinds of myth, all that, wasn't it? Did one need those myths? Were they necessary, to borrow one of the Reverend Davies's cherished phrases which he would flourish at all opportune and some inopportune moments, for "living unto righteousness"?

He thought, of course, that here was a dilemma newly discovered by himself. Well, himself and a few others, perhaps. Only gradually did it creep in upon him that he was not unique. This or something like it, had been bothering a lot of people for a long time. Perhaps even the Reverend Davies. Hence his agitation at the prospect of looking outside the Great Myth under which he sheltered.

And then Russell had written a single question on an otherwise blank page. It struck him now as pretty obvious. There it was still, spread across the paper, when he hesitated at the age of fifty over pages of that old notebook wondering whether to rip them out and burn them.

Myths only attempts at explanation?

By the time he met Editha Wirz while he was doing his National Service in Germany, every day had become a tussle with explanation. But explanation, he by then felt, was entirely tied up with actually living. There was no point in demythologising if it didn't clear a way to living with a kind of directness which myths got in the way of. When he had seen her standing as he passed the church in the nearby village one day with her skirt blowing against her thighs, his pang of desire was not simply a young man's helpless prurience. It was desire for the entire fullness of life.

But then when he thought of all that, how she had so utterly *pledged* herself to him, how they had talked, how rapt, how keenly that whole inter-involvement of how to explain things, and living with utter conviction, had exercised the two of them in their coming together in the little they ever saw of each other, and then how he had simply packed up his few things and left (oh yes, he had said he would be back for her) and after a while never even written to her again – well, how did *that* square with those preposterous ideas in his notebook, with any notion of perfectibility, of living unto righteousness? *There* was a blatant enough failure to live up to anything.

It was in 1956, wasn't it, when he met her, about the time of the Suez crisis? Rumours around the R.A.F. camp, each rapidly revised by some other, about who would and who wouldn't be sent off to take part. Never any word from above, as far as he could recall, just what one read in the papers and heard on the news, but of course that was how it always was. Everybody had been sure that some of them would have to go. Probably not him, he would be needed where he was, performing his trite routines with phones and flight-plans. There had always seemed something unreal about it all. He sat there taking and making phone calls, listening to phantom pilots jabbering on the radio channels, watching radar screens, and none of it, in fact none of anything his National Service involved – stamping about on parade squares, setting the corporal on the firing range screaming ("It takes bleeding *genius* to miss *every* time, airman!"), standing in his "bedspace" for kit inspection, wearing that graceless uniform which seemed to belong more to the world of his childhood when half the crowd on any street would be wearing blue or khaki, and which he got out of at every opportunity – none of it had seemed to have much to do with real life. He had started to read *The Trial*, trying the German text, *Der Prozess*, alongside Edwin Muir's Penguin translation. Yes, Kafkaesque, what a useful word that was! A world without whys and wherefores. *Real* life with its whys and wherefores was the Germany outside the camp, the Germany of the post-war economic miracle, the Germany still traced and incised by those hugely real events of his childhood. *Real* life was Editha Wirz.

And by 1980, when those days occasionally fell into his mind, which wasn't often because he was far too busy running around trying to keep himself and the business above water, George Raciuk's business though it might be, or to come up with any explanations at all – but late at night perhaps when over a Scotch something would suddenly make him remember a detail or two like the time he and Editha had gone together to a concert in Düsseldorf and heard – what was it? Wilhelm Kempff playing Beethoven? – he asked himself a question. In what sense had *he* simply packed up and left *her*? She could have come with him. He had wanted her to. But no, she just didn't seem able to do that. To pull up her roots, or however one might put it. A lot to ask, of course, but then, how she had *pledged* herself. And wasn't this sort of thing *supposed* to be about asking a lot? Once, six months or so after he'd last seen her, a letter arrived saying she often thought she would simply get on a train and come, but when she thought clearly, she felt somehow it was just now not yet the right time. They must be sensible for a short while, and they would certainly be rewarded with "great happiness" – *viel Glück*. They must just have faith in it happening. And then nothing was said again. But after all, what did thinking *clearly* mean? If she'd really looked right through the thing, she'd have seen that something held her back against everything she claimed to want. In some corner of herself, she was not sure, she was afraid. That had to be it.

*

So when did they start going there? For weekends, sometimes for whole weeks, whenever they had enough time off classes? Sitting in the Poonah Balti House and Tandoori in 1993 – it wasn't so easy to all get together nowadays – the four of them gave it a re-run.

"Well, as you know, I first met Kingston *before* Sussex. It was some sort of wannabe-swinging coffee bar somewhere up Paddington way," offered Sarah Jenkins, Brownlee as she then was. "He insisted on walking me back to Paddington underground, said it wasn't too safe round there. I was only just sixteen."

"Sixteen! Were we *ever* that age?"

"I was, you probably never were, Russell. We all know you had no youth, just came fully adult into the world."

"Well, it can be supposed I *did* have a youth. But by the time I met all of you in Brighton, I was twenty-seven, remember."

He had gone to Sussex University as a so-called "mature student". He afterwards often reflected that "mature" was a relative term.

"God, how did we do it? In the snow sometimes, no proper bathroom, no proper heating, just that big woodstove which Kingston and Paula had to cook on and everything!"

"Yeah, the Aga. The legendary Aga of mayonnaise fame."

A pause while they jointly stared, as if deciphering occult runes, at the yellow curry-stains on the white tablecloth. Kingston and Paula, the other two of the six, not now seen for years.

"Ho, ho," – Michael Jenkins ending the silence – "Remembrance of things past!"

Actually, *he* hadn't witnessed the mayonnaise, only its aftermath.

"Why for Christ's sake did we all keep going back there?"

He poured himself another glass of wine and forgot, so struck was he by the force of his own question, to pass the bottle round the table.

"Well, my sweet," said Sarah, "As far as my memory serves me, you were as keen as any of us. A model for the undermining of bourgeois society, didn't you used to say?"

"Christ! Did we really say such things in those days?"

"Of course we did," said Russell. "Nowadays we only feel them. That is, none of us would go back to precisely anything like that, I take it. But we feel we weren't entirely … weren't essentially wrong."

"We feel scared maybe?" suggested Sarah.

"Scared?" Camilla, as always, not letting *that* kind of thing by.

"Oh well, Cam love, we know not you. Anyway, it was lovely in summer out there."

No Camilla, not you, Russell was thinking. You *still* say those things. Just learned new ways of wrapping them up. The new newspeak. Except with me, thank God. Presentational skills, they call it nowadays. And those you certainly have. I never did.

"Barlett's Cottage. Remember we always wondered why it was called that? Asked one or two people round about. We never did find out. 'Bloody students,' you could see them thinking."

"As Mary Sturgess would have said, 'One looks for explanations.'" Camilla, typically, underlining. Then, pensively: "And none of it would have happened if it hadn't been for Kingston in the first place ...."

"Of course," said Sarah. "Finding the place, way out there past Lewes down that dirt track. Then getting Paula to rent it in her name."

Paula's accent went down well with Estate Agents, better for Kingston not to show himself. She had paid the deposit too. Well, she could always get cash out of her mother. "Good old Mater, wallowing in it," Kingston used to say.

Her father had been one of those ineffable somethings-in-the-city. He had had his massive heart attack when Paula was twelve.

"Remember you used to have to get off the bus the stop after the *Cricketers' Arms*. If you missed that request stop it was half-a-mile to walk back. Lugging our sleeping bags and everything." As she spoke, Sarah stared meditatively into her empty wine glass. At last, her husband filled it.

"Well, the question was, wasn't it, which year was it?"

Camilla, getting back to the point. As had always been her way, thought Russell, at times found tiresome by the others. But necessary, they always had to concede. And he asked himself for the several thousandth time, what would I have done without her? They'd only met again those few years previously, but it seemed like always it was only she had held his life in place.

"I took my stuff out there to swot for second-year exams, I remember," he said. "In peace and quiet in the depths of the countryside ...."

"Jeez, Russell, with Kingston and Paula around?" put in Mike, his accent turning up a notch. "That is, when he hadn't packed her off to scrounge something else from her mother. Remember the way Kingston mimicked 'Mater' as he called her?"

"Well, anyway, second year, that must have been … sixty-five?"

Yes, four years after he'd come back from roughing it on the continent following his National Service. Somehow, the whole thing with Editha had just slipped away, water between his fingers. Then there'd been Camilla, and then there wasn't.

*

Of course, there had been others between Editha and Camilla. Really, he could hardly remember them. Not their faces, not how their voices sounded. That was the difference between Editha and Camilla and the others. A little bit perhaps about their bodies even if not much had happened.

It was the series of full stops that had stuck in his mind. Yes, she had come somewhere between Editha and Camilla. Phoebe – that was her name wasn't it? *Could* it have been? Made you think of milkmaids. Hadn't most people called her Phee?

Anyway, all he really recalled was her "wanting to thank him." What for? For a year of very great happiness, she said. *Viel Glück.* Even then he had thought, what could *very great* happiness mean? Seemed ripe for a bit of demythologizing, that.

He wasn't to think she gave up such a friendship lightly, or without thinking.

They all said something like that, but it didn't stop them giving it up.

What they really needed from each other only hurt the other by its incompleteness.

Well, yes, he remembered her saying that, and not understanding what she meant.

Afterwards he thought perhaps she meant sex. Odd that. "You don't really want me, do you?" she said after one evening in his room. And looking back, he realized he didn't.

She had been quite tall and strongly built. He couldn't have described her face afterwards, but recalled thinking of it as like a ballerina's, and she wore her nearly black hair in a long ponytail. But she wasn't lithe enough, perhaps, for a ballerina.

That was Phee. The card she wrote afterwards, "thanking" him again. Ending with the series of full stops …. Ellipsis points, his supervisor called those when he started doing his thesis. Something left out, something unexplained. Something inexplicable?

But that last letter from Camilla, now. There'd been the meeting in London about six months after they'd left university, and then that last letter. Sometimes he'd thought perhaps he shouldn't have left it unanswered. But whenever it came into his mind and he asked himself why he had just let her drift into history, he could only suppose that at the time he hadn't really *wanted* things the way she did. Or couldn't cope with that way. Or to be more precise, he had wanted other things more. She walked off from Sussex with a First. Not that she didn't work damn hard for it, never seen anybody go at things like her. But would have got a good degree whatever.

Yet then, the fact of the matter was, he hadn't found somewhere he could stop and say, this is it, this is a fixture, until he'd run into Camilla again at that conference in 1987. There she'd been, speaking, taking questions, dazzling. It wasn't quite how he remembered her back in the days when they'd crammed into a shared sleeping-bag at Bartlett's Cottage. Not quite, but it was the same Camilla, all right. Of course, it had been his failure. She wasn't going to let him hold her back, then. Now she didn't have to worry. But Christ, after she'd been married to that high-powered bloke at the L.S.E. Seems the marriage simply ran out of steam when he was head-hunted by somewhere or other in the States. And then to bump into her like that, and the business about done-for, one of the knock-on casualties of the Thatcher cuts. Schools and colleges didn't have the cash any more, and what with languages not being taught as they used to be …. Well, he'd never been a proper businessman. Camilla just sat and laughed when he first said that to her. She shook her head and laughed. "Whom are you telling *that*?" she said. Then she said: "I'm laughing out of relief, really, you know. Thank God! I haven't got to be afraid you've changed."

He still didn't quite know how she did it. So adroit at manipulating the new newspeak that people often took her for the arch-moderniser. Nothing to do with "spin", she'd be indignant if they tried to imply that. *That* had got to the ludicrous point, she came to say, where the spin itself was to label any pronouncement you wanted to rubbish "spin". Funny term, when you thought of the old figures of speech involving spin. Being in a spin about something. Spinning a yarn, telling a pack of whoppers. Funny how it had caught on so.

No, she said, people had always wanted to varnish the truth, paper over the cracks. The point was, there'd been a systemic shift in the way things are felt and perceived. It was all part of a sense that you couldn't talk in the same way about things. It happens every so often. But it was precisely always the whoppers, the propensity in mankind toward deceiving and being deceived, that she always had her sights on. Because the enemy doesn't change, she said. Just changes its camouflage. Like one of those viruses they think they've zapped and then find it's mutated.

He'd said something about the fin-de-siècle, end of the millennium which it wasn't but never mind, the mythic power of numbers, people wanting to believe that when numbers change things are different.

"Well, of course there'll be a field day for all the windbags and self-appointed pundits when 2000 looms. But the goodies and baddies are still the same. The ideological sands shift, but you have to keep redrawing the line in the same place in the sand. Like it's still the same for you and me, the same as it was at the beginning, despite all the things that ...."

"Despite everything. Systemic shifts or whatever."

Everything that looks and feels different. Which was why he could sit at home in Camilla's very-nice-thankyou apartment in front of the word processor doing what he should always have been doing. Translating Heinrich Böll.

*

Camilla Reeves sat in the dusty room above a pub near St. Giles-in-the-Fields. You got to it by taking the tube to Tottenham Court Road and going a bit down Charing Cross Road and then along Denmark Street. Tin Pan Alley, people sometimes called it. Really, she hadn't any time for all that commercialized junk. *Music* for Christ's sake. Of course, this was a subject she'd always had to keep off with Kingston. There'd been that argument once, got close to out of hand. So easy-going, Kingston, you could say what you liked to him, but not on that one point, she discovered to her cost. Russell and the others had always steered her away from it afterwards.

But she'd done a piece in *Tribune* about it. Crucial to make the distinction between *popular* culture, the culture of the people, she'd written, and mass exploitation by commercial interests. In later years, she was amused when she thought of how she had written like that. She turned her hand to the new cultural theory with ease, perceived clearly how to manipulate what Russell liked to call (because he knew the patness of *that* amused her) the new newspeak.

"That's *you* writes those pieces in *Tribune*?" people said to her. Bloody insulting. True she was less than a year out of university, only twenty-three. To them, probably, because she wore high boots and miniskirt and her hair like Julie Christie in *Darling* she looked like some mindless bird in the audience of a Beatles concert. Take them, now, the Beatles. Ordinary Liverpool lads, real popular talent there, people said. Innovative sound, a kind of ballad-like poetry in the lyrics, caught the feeling of the moment. Well O.K., interesting, but Christ, hadn't that modicum of talent been blown up! And why? Because somebody had seen money in it.

Great living in London, despite how Mum and Dad might keep on about whether she was coping. All happening here. Of course, Mum and Dad down there in Suffolk …. Dad fussing about whether to put his tomatoes out yet last time she spoke to them on the phone. Mum with her "How long's that job in London for then, dear? Plenty of nice jobs round here, you know."

Camilla never really thought about the name they had saddled her with until she came across Cam Ramsay in *To the Lighthouse*. It was on the reading list at university.

Her parents wouldn't have known who Virginia Woolf was. They hardly ever went outside Suffolk, thought it a dreadful long way (but the war was different, you had to put up with such things) for her father to have to go when he was stationed for a time near Aberdeen. There when she was born. Her mother had always been fond of camellias – *camillas*, she pronounced them like that – and her father grew them for her. Her mates at school had called her Cam or Cammie. Sometimes there had been taunts about Camiknickers, but even as a small girl Camilla had wielded a resourceful tongue, and she soon saw off the jokers and would-be bullies.

Then when she discovered the book she had read it several times. Cam became for her the centre of it. The wild villain Cam, Cam the Wicked, who wouldn't behave to order. Cam who thought they must fight tyranny to the death, who reverenced justice most of all human qualities. Yes, she said, when Mary quizzed her, she knew that Cam wasn't exactly the *centre* of the book, that was a distortion. But it didn't change how she felt.

Laurence Thomson was the speaker this evening. Member of the new Greater London Council, talking about how it compares so far with the old L.C.C. Good bloke for her union branch to have got. Very much on the left of the Labour Party. She'd suggested him to the committee, of course.

"Not surprisingly, there's an element of confusion," he said. "These much larger voting units than we had with the old L.C.C. and other county councils have bound into them an anti-democratic element. How can individuals feel they are being properly represented?"

One way of making the individual's voice felt, Camilla thought, was by being in the Union. But didn't think white-collar workers needed a union, some of them at the office. Unions only for the hoi-polloi. Not having much success getting them to come along to these meetings. Not getting that right somehow, though her approach to people had been good, so everybody said, as secretary of the Socialist Society at Sussex. Different world, that, though. Have to think about that if she did eventually go into politics like she'd often thought she would. Keep that option open, along with others, time yet, though mustn't take too long about it. Part of Russell's trouble, takes too long about everything, won't ever get anywhere much if he doesn't look out. Perhaps just not ambitious. Suppose I am, have to admit it. Perhaps must try to tone it down a bit at the office, though, puts some of them off. Think I'm a cocky youngster, I can see that. That woman Samantha, snapped my head off the other day, oh shut up, Camilla, such a damn Bolshy, you are. Cam the Wicked. Best not to answer. More senior than me, after all.

"The argument about the need to regroup and reconstruct was, of course, seductive. There was a certain superficial truth in it. But in fact what has happened? We have a G.L.C. representing eight-and-a-half million people as against an L.C.C. representing three million. The number of representatives per person has been *reduced*. We councillors each represent much too large an area. We can't deal with people's worries and concerns on anything like an individual basis. The interests of the *people* have not really been served."

A point he keeps coming back to that. The interests of the people. Of course, he's right. That's what's paramount. Start off at the bottom if she did go into politics. Local borough council. Then perhaps move on to GLC, like him.

Only trouble with these meetings the way this Keith has latched on to me. Sitting next to me now, on these awful old chairs, must be wartime Utility or something. Oh well, he's OK. Wants to sleep with me of course. Can see what *his* interests are. Hasn't said so yet, but working up to it. I might, see how things develop. Nice enough body he's got. No comparison with Russell, goes without saying. Still, if Russell doesn't want to keep in touch, there's no point in me keep chasing him. Haven't got time anyway. Lovely man, though. Best it's ever been, those few times with him, even though he's a bit of a fumbler. Cautious sort, doesn't matter. Nicer really, gentler. Oh, hark at me, as if I've had dishes of experience and can make comparisons. How many times have I ever had *it*, after all? Properly, that is. More times with Russell than with anybody else, that's for certain. How many years older than me, and still a student? Takes too long over everything. Had to start him off on his essays even. Damn good once he got started but agonised too much, never got through all his workload. Had to tell him, no good expecting *perfection* in this world.

Suppose he'll just be something in my past.

This Laurence Thompson is a nice-looking man. Tall, nicely built, open intelligent face, lots of character in it. How old? Classic touch of grey at the temples. Fortyish. Saw him glancing at my legs. Keep off there, though. There'll be a wife, or at least somebody, and his position to think of. One-night stand? No, silly. Keep right out of that sort of thing, don't want it.

"The GLC must in future be prepared to take a strong stand. The need for attention to the comprehensive school system is urgent. The provision of day nurseries is more important in London than anywhere."

That was something Laurence Thomson said which was to bounce back at Camilla later. When she got pregnant by Keith, so stupid that, she hadn't really wanted him at all, just this need to push up against the edges, to defy the old taboos. In the air, all that sort of idea. Looked like her job wasn't just a matter of ambition any more but necessity. Yes, a nightmare it would be, trying to find a decent crèche and the nursery accommodation.

"But planning and development is going to be the key question. We have to face the fact that planning has *not* always been the LCC's strength."

Planning the world. Planning your own life. Could one, should one? At Sussex they had wanted her to stay and do a Master's. But there's a real world out here. Mary had tried to persuade her. Smashing woman, Dr. Mary Sturgess, mind like a razor. Occam's razor, she taught us about that. "Well, Camilla, you can always come back later. You know you'd always be welcome. Anyway, make sure you come down and see me. I'll put you up for the weekend, you'll need to get out of London sometimes." Been down once already, lovely. Want to keep her as a friend. Ought to go and see Mum and Dad, keep putting it off.

There her parents had lived, down there, through half-a-century of struggle for change. Her father didn't *quite* still touch his forelock to the Squire but it wasn't much better than that. She had given up suggesting to them that they were in the perpetual possession of being well-deceived, it only upset them, and fuelled their view, which in their kindliness (and after all, she was a "grown girl" now) they tried to disguise from her, of her contrariness. They would never understand that she wasn't coming back home. Never really understand that she had work to do.

Oh, what's Keith nudging me for now? Wants me to ask a question about planning, thinks I know something about it. Just an excuse to get his anatomy against mine, really.

Years later, when Thatcher scuppered the G.L.C., the whole of Thomson's talk came back into Camilla's mind. How odd, that he had been saying those things back then, and everything seemed now to have looped back to *before* that! It would all have to be said again, all that work done over again. And some time, however far ahead, something like the G.L.C. would have to be resurrected. After all, despite his worries, it had to be said that because of its sheer size the Council had presented a real obstacle to the Thatcher agenda, at a time when most other opposition had been neutralized. So much so, that the woman felt impelled to take extreme measures. Yes. True, the G.L.C. in the end hadn't been able to stand up to her. But look, Camilla would say to her "inner circle" as the eighties turned into the nineties. All that builds up. The received view is that Thatcherism has left its permanent mark, and there's some truth in that. On the other hand, slowly, slowly, it's dawning on people that that's not the only way. Each grain of sand builds up resistance. Like the pearl in the oyster, if you don't mind the cliché. We can capitalise on that, if we go about it rightly.

And that about planning, too, had taken on an ironic edge when she found herself pregnant. Yet the miscarriage had been a kind of disappointment, even though it solved a lot of problems. No more wasting energy debating whether she should look up Keith again and *tell* him. She didn't want him around, but shouldn't he *know*?

She'd been working too hard, doing too much, the doctor said. Pissed you off, doctors, the way they thought they could tell you how to live your life. What about you, she felt like saying, work hard, don't you, pack a lot in? Males, though, don't have miscarriages.

*

When Sergeant Alexander Hanslope left the Royal Air Force in 1937, he received a *Statement of Discharge of an Airman's Qualifications and Employment* (Form 856A). Russell came across it as he shuffled through his mother's papers after her death in 1994, a roll of quality cartridge paper that looked trying to pass itself off for parchment. Signed by Group Captain J.C. Cartwright, Officer i/c Records.

> A very fine all round pilot, both by day and night, with approximately 2,100 hours experience on single engined aircraft; accurate, knowledgable and conscientious, and an excellent test pilot. He is also an exceptionally good instructor, whose aerobatics are outstandingly smooth, and who has demonstrated by practical work his suitability for the highest category. In his basic trade of Carpenter Rigger, of which he possessed a sound knowledge, he has given every satisfaction.

Alexander had begun his working life at the age of fifteen, following his father into the trade, as an apprentice carpenter. But Alexander's reports from Board School recorded his exceptionally high marks in Mathematics and English and commented on his unusual academic abilities. "For a boy of his background" was left unstated, and the foreman in his workshop one day made a pointed reference to people with "ideas above their station". He knew that his family could not afford further education for him. No matter, he must take things into his own hands. After only a cursory consultation with his father, he had manoeuvred his bicycle out of the garden shed one late summer Sunday in 1921, and set out for Portsmouth. It was here that his Uncle Cyril lived. Before retirement, Uncle Cyril had reached the rank of Chief Petty Officer in the Royal Navy. Alexander was not too young to form the judgement that Cyril Hanslope might well have attained a higher naval rank had he been of the "right background." Of all his relatives, Uncle Cyril was the one to whom Alexander felt he could talk with some certainty that what he was after would be properly understood.

A brief correspondence with his Uncle and his Aunt Maisie had already brought an invitation to stay overnight, the next day being August Bank Holiday. The evening's chat which followed included Alexander's initiation into his Uncle's rum ration. Yes, of course, said Uncle Cyril, Alex was just the sort of likely young fellow the Services were looking out for. The war, you know, it opened all our eyes. This is just the time, brain wanted more than brawn nowadays, a new age dawning. All sorts of technical innovations. Well, Cyril knew what he was talking about. His cruiser had been sunk at the Battle of Jutland, and on recovery he'd been trained in the firing of depth charges. One of the outcomes of that battle, you know, he said, the German navy more or less out of the way, but we had to have means of countering their U-boats. But look here, the navy not quite as much at the forefront of these things as the Royal – what d'you call it now? – Royal Flying Corps in my day. Flying, *that's* the future. Any future war – which Heaven forbid, but this Versailles treaty, I don't like the look of it, more trouble up ahead if you ask me – will be fought to a very great extent in the air. And even if, which God grant, we really do have peace, flying is the coming thing. Who knows, one of these days your generation will be getting into aeroplanes as a matter of course the way you get on your bicycle or into the omnibus now. You couldn't do better, Alex. Look, I cut this out from the *News Chronicle* the other day. An announcement by the Royal Air Force – that's it, dammit – of their scheme for competitive entry to trade apprenticeships. Write off about it, young feller, as soon as you get home. You can pen a pretty letter, I know that from the ones you've sent us. Straight away, old chap. Now, you can manage just another tot, can't you? Come on lad, put hairs on your chest. Oh leave off, Maisie m'dear, he's *not* still only a boy.

Just over a year later, Alexander began serving his apprenticeship in the School of Technical Training at Halton. He had passed the Air Ministry examination in mathematics, science, English and a general paper, and waited for the admissible age of entry. It had been no surprise to be offered the trade of Carpenter Rigger. He had been, said the Statement of Discharge, "capable of carrying out all work connected with the rigging and truing-up of wooden aircraft, and of the repair and manufacture of all timber parts of aircraft in replacement of those broken or damaged." He had "a thorough knowledge of stresses and strains imposed on airframes, the theory of flight and general principles of aircraft design, and a ground engineer's understanding of the technicalities of the machine."

It was now simply a question of getting into one of those machines and taking it *off* the ground. Which one day, on invitation from his slightly older friend Pilot-Sergeant Reg Machin, he did. He climbed into the seat in front of Sergeant Machin, and took the thing up. No need for Machin to tell him what to do, he had the instinct, Machin said, more than anybody else he'd seen. And a few months later, on the recommendation of his commanding officer after a few words from Machin, he was at Central Flying School.

The Statement was dated the same month Russell was born. Alexander, perhaps having his new responsibility in mind, took up civilian flying. But history intervened just two years later. Back in the R.A.F., Russell's father got an immediate commission, and sailed up through the echelons. Already Wing Commander when he was shot down in '44.

"It was something I had in common with Paula," Russell said to Camilla, as she helped him sort through his mother's belongings. "I never really knew him, I suppose. So this, this piece of paper ...."

"Is some kind of help in knowing him?"

"Well ... what might your friend Mary say? 'Any such document is a manner of narrative practice, like any other.' Does it mean I *know* him any better?"

"But not like any other *for you*. Mary would say that too. But wait." She put her hand on his arm. "*Machin*, did you say? Air-Vice-Marshall Machin? I had to go and see him once. Something to do with that report I helped do, you know, I co-authored it, civilian alternatives .... No, of course, you weren't around then. He'd be about the same vintage, about the age your father would have been. Well, there you are!"

Certainly it was a help for Camilla. A clarifying. She saw it all at once, though in that way which meant she'd always known. The day his mother got the telegram about his father was the day on which Russell, child though he was, stopped trusting life.

Even when he had *her* secure and forever, he would never quite clear his mind of that distrust.

*

It had been Kingston who had got Russell into the business. He didn't see a lot of Kingston these days: there had been that bit of a breach between Kingston and the others after the Test Match. But they always had some means of contact, and occasionally they would run into each other. Kingston had fixed up the meeting with George Racuik, and only afterwards phoned Russell, woken him up at around half-past-midnight to tell him. He knew this bloke who knew a bloke. Well, Kingston always did. Russell was still fiddling at his thesis on Heinrich Böll. Five years he'd been at it, doing whatever job was more or less tolerable to keep his head above water. The water flowed under the bridge all the same, taking with it Patsy and Thora, who had registered, well, a bit less marginally in his consciousness than ellipsis-points Phee. No, after Camilla there had never been anyone with whom he could stop and say, this is it. But of course there had been these others, as indeterminate as his work on his thesis.

The bloke known by Kingston's bloke had a girlfriend who worked for George Racuik. She was some sort of a general clerical assistant and secretary. And another bloke, the one they had who had been doing the German side of things, had unexpectedly got a job with Insel Verlag. They needed somebody who knew German and at least something about books. They were a small specialist set-up and couldn't pay anybody much, let alone anybody who had the kind of expertise the job really called for.

He had phoned Kingston back the next day and told him to call the meeting off. Kingston was jamming all afternoon and at a gig all evening, but he finally answered the phone around, again, half-past-midnight.

"O.K., just trying to be nice, man, we go back after all, you and me, and I just thought this might be cool for you if only for a bit. What else you doing, heh man? But have it your own way. You got the address and number anyway if you change your mind. Think about it, man."

Russell thought about it for two weeks. Be nice to have a regular income. Perhaps worth looking into it at least. Then he thought, two weeks, they'll have got somebody else by now, no point bothering. Typical, Camilla would have said (but she wasn't around to say it.) She would have said: "How did you get produced by a dad who flew planes like nobody's business and must have been decisive about things?" "Don't know," he would have said. "I didn't really know *him*, did I?" The exchange or something like it was to become one of their rhetorical clinchings, one of their ways of underwriting their togetherness.

Another week later, he got a screed from his supervisor asking for a raft of changes to the chapter of his thesis which, after a long gap, he'd sent in. He picked up the phone and somebody called Jenny – must be the girlfriend, he supposed – arranged for him to go and see "George" the next day.

He went. Up the narrow bare stairs, and into George Racuik's "office". Powerful aroma of cheap cigars. Over the top of piles of books, George's face and bald head. Like a pumpkin at Hallowe'en with one of those great curved smiles gashed into it. Must have been pushing sixty-five already. No window in the little box of a room, just a high small skylight. When the room some years later became his own, Russell climbed up on a chair and opened the skylight in fine weather. He had to use force the first time. The smell of cigars never entirely disappeared. He didn't ever see George open it. George didn't much care for fresh air. Perhaps it was that he'd had his fill of it sleeping in ditches and God knows what during the war. Some kind of courier with the Resistance, he'd been, even getting to London in the thick of it all a few times. Nor, in George's time, was the cleaning firm which came in once a week – George couldn't afford daily – ever allowed to touch the "office".

But after five minutes, Russell thought he'd never met a nicer man. They saw eye-to-eye immediately. In fifteen minutes Russell had accepted the job, before any such immaterialities as working-hours or salary were even mentioned. At some point during the afternoon, which evolved into cheap cigars and nips of some arcane brandy-liqueur and a long chat about Heinrich Böll, a figure was mentioned. It floated off into a smoky corner of the room and never came down again. The eventual reality, which only Jenny seemed to have any knowledge of, was nowhere near it.

Russell fell easily into the job. There was George, upstairs, "running" the place. George, Russell discovered, had first gone to work there in the early nineteen-fifties. The then owner became his father-in-law, and he inherited the business. Somehow, for people who knew what they wanted, he could always supply it. He seemed to have a working knowledge of nearly every European language and of the publishing business right across the continent, even across in those days the divide of East and West. He'd only delegated the German stuff in the first place because somebody suitable had turned up and it left him free to deal with the rest. Then there was Jenny behind a kind of counter in a corner of the downstairs stockroom with a couple of filing cabinets and an electric typewriter. Eventually, Russell got a cheap deal on a computer for her through Sarah – she and Mike seemed somehow to divide their working lives almost equally between here and Australia – and even managed to get Sarah to come over for the best part of three days to show them how to computerize. She didn't charge anything. Could have made a lot of money in those three days. Russell had his own corner between shelves in the first-floor stockroom. Neither "stockroom" was much bigger than a front room in an ordinary house. There was Les who came in three hours every morning regular and punctual, and Liz for three erratic hours most afternoons. They did the orders. Les was Lesley and came in immediately she'd taken her three kids to school; Liz was Liston and was an actor more or less permanently "filling in" between "work". It was Jenny started called him Liz. "Jennifer *dear*, do you *mind*? A little gender confusion does nobody any harm, but there are *limits*!" He loved it. Days he failed to turn up, Jenny and Russell did his orders.

That was the "firm". Working hours never having been stipulated, at first Russell came and went when he liked. But after a couple of years or so George began dragging himself in from home less than every day because of his whatever-it-was the doctors couldn't quite pin down. "Also, was meinen sie, diese Ärzte?" he said one day when Russell had gone to his house to talk a few things over. He was speaking English less these days, reverting to the tongues of his earlier days. "It's life, it's history, taken their toll, that's all that's wrong with me. No cure for that." Russell's coming gradually got earlier because there was always something urgently needed seeing to, and going extended sometimes to ten o'clock at night. When George stopped doing much at all, Russell tried to find somebody else who might fit in, but it was hopeless for what he could offer even part-time. He never did finish the thesis. When he moved in with Camilla he got it out again and looked it over to see if anything could be salvaged and brought up to date, written up as an article. "What you are is like that phrase in the Larkin poem," Camilla said. "A scholar *manqué*, that's what you are."

Running any kind of business, it had never been what Russell had thought of himself doing. Jenny helped as best she could with the accounts and paperwork but even she wasn't properly qualified. What's more, she'd given up the bloke that knew Kingston's bloke and seemed at a bit of a loose end. Kept asking Russell to come out to lunch with her. She'd leave little packets of things she knew he liked on his desk, once even half-a-dozen bottles of wine …. Talked sometimes about going over to see her "cousins and whatnot, all of them over there." Had Russell ever been to the Caribbean? He ought to, he'd like it …. She could take him around if he liked …. No, he said, he didn't think he'd really like it, he and hot climates didn't agree, he'd found that out when he went out to see Mike in Australia, and anyway, what about the business?

"You never knew Kingston, did you?" He'd asked her this several times before, but the subject seemed to get brushed aside.

"No. Heard Jimmy talk about him. But I never met him."

"He's over there now." Russell only knew this because he'd got a gaudy postcard several months before. "I get the impression he might be there for some time."

Odd contrast between the tacky picture on that postcard and Kingston's few lines of meticulous italic handwriting on the other side. He had always written like that, all his student essays, everything. One of those things about Kingston. All the few lines said was more or less what Russell had told Jenny. And an address. Russell knew what that meant. It was Kingston's encrypting of "this is where I'm at, man, and don't say I didn't tell you."

"Great, Kingston. Bit crazy, though, over the top sometimes."

"Like all of *us*, you mean?"

"Oh, Jenny! I didn't ...."

But she only laughed. That deep chuckle of hers descending down the scale, it kept the place cheerful. Without her, the whole set-up would collapse anyway.

And of course it was hopeless, in the long run. When Russell met Camilla again he had already started negotiations on George's behalf with a couple of possible buyers. He hoped Jenny would be able to keep the job. Probably, though, a buyer would just cherry-pick the parts of the business they wanted and then shut the place down. It was all that would make sense.

Every time he heard that laugh of Jenny's, it reminded him of Kingston.

*

There Camilla was, just wrapped up her session at the conference. She was standing with her back to him, in an intent huddle of four or five people, all gesticulating, waving papers in their hands.

Over the years, what some censoring device in Russell's consciousness had always blocked out was any knowledge of Camilla's life now. She was ever there, however fugitively, like a phone number on the pad which never got called. But it was unthinkable, any effort to find out what she was doing. where she was. He couldn't talk to Kingston about her, it was always a kind of skirting around things with Kingston, especially those days at Sussex. It was only from Mike once that he'd heard anything.

When Mike had been back in Melbourne for a couple of years, Sarah went out and they got married. The idea had started to get a hold in Russell's mind of a "business-trip-cum-a-few-days-holiday", as he phrased it to George. Mike and Sarah would put him up so it would only be a question of the air ticket. He would look into possible openings over there, he vaguely supposed, for the business. There was nothing vague about George's perception that Russell just needed a break, and he stumped up most of the fare.

The day after he arrived, he and Mike had got off the tram by the Post Office in Elizabeth Street. Mike was taking him to have a look at the city centre. In Russell's pocket were the few names and addresses he had managed to scratch up of people connected with the foreign-language book trade. They crossed the Bourke Street Mall and headed down towards the river and the Arts Centre. But it was hot like Russell had never known. Jesus, Russell, Mike said, get yourself a pair of shorts. And suddenly, just before the Block Arcade, he was diving down some steps off the street. Russell followed him down and into some kind of subterranean bar. The strip-lighting in the ceiling was excessively bright and the maroon-vinyl furnishing was excessively shiny. And for any view of the city it was a non-starter. But it was air-conditioned, and one cold beer after another stretched into the afternoon. "Thirty-eight degrees or something now," Mike said. "Hottest time of the day, we don't want to be out there now. Not unusual in February. When I was a kid, we used to fry eggs on the pavement." He looked at Russell with that compressed set of the mouth and slightly closed eyes that Russell had known when they were students. It always turned into a grin. In a long drawl, he just said: "Y-e-a-h." But then, because all that was just a preamble: "You know, don't you, Camilla's divorced?"

Russell never did get the pair of shorts, and nor did he do any business, but he came back with more tan than Jenny had ever seen on him, a slightly distant look in his eyes, and a taste for Aussie reds.

He hadn't even known Camilla was married.

Now, in the conference hall, he moved a little nearer to her, discreetly; hovered. A few people edged past him, nodded or smiled. A face he recognised on the other side of the hall, oh yes, Bill Gallagher of Inscape Inc., thought he was back in Seattle, must be over here again. Gallagher caught sight of him and raised a hand in acknowledgement. But he too was deep in consultation with somebody.

Yes, thought Russell, it's often like this. I *know* people and yet I don't know them. Of course, they'll count me in, make themselves agreeable, later on in the bar as long as I buy my rounds. Then we'll go away from here and I might as well not exist for all I'll hear from them – well, only when they want something they really *can't* get anywhere else. And it came sharply into his mind how even back then at Bartlett's Cottage, Camilla knew. What had she said once? – what they'd been talking about he didn't remember, probably it was one of those times she'd started him going on some assignment. Somehow she could always see, straight away, the way into a thing.

"You're so *tentative*, Russell. You doubt everything, doubt yourself even."

Mike used to call her Schoolmam Cam. Or Right-On Reeves. She herself preferred Cam the Wicked.

Should he push with her, now? Walk into the middle of that little thicket of intensity and just say – well, say what?

Somebody in Camilla's huddle said: "OK then, four this afternoon, Camilla", and somebody else, walking away: "You *have* got my email address ….?"

"Yes, yes," she said, pivotting on the sole of one foot, her eyes following the speaker, her body turning towards Russell. "Hello …." he began to say.

"Russell."

They stood, unmoving, a few yards from each other. Voices crooned and figures flitted around them, but they were not part of it.

She just said, again: "Russell".

For a moment – she only became fully conscious of it when she thought about the moment afterwards – Camilla relived that abortive last meeting in London. She'd shrugged it off at the time, had felt she had to. But what was all that which had been going on since? The years went into fast-rewind. Her children, but what else? All that going on, but there had always been an ellipsis, something inexplicably not there. She had left it somewhere and never gone back for it, never had time.

To Russell it seemed that she had been talking incessantly for the last two hours, ever since he walked into the hall. Now she was speechless. Camilla! Speechless!

Then they both started together:

"Well, a blast from the past ...."

"A long time, Camilla, how ...."

They both laughed.

She stepped across the yard or so separating them and put one hand on his arm. Was it to feel whether he was *real*?

"Russell," she said again.

*

It was at only the second meeting with Camilla after this that the Test Match came up. Russell had hardly given it a thought for years. The Test Match had been what the two of them had come to call it. Now, it had to be talked about, acknowledged. After that, it would just stay in the footnotes.

At Sussex Kingston had been the sort that ended up with a Second without visibly having done any work. He'd hand in his essays in that effortless, immaculate handwriting five minutes before the deadline and get them back with a B minus. To see him strolling into an exam. room was to understand precisely why the expression laid-back had been coined. Sometimes, when he condescended to attend lectures, the posture became literal. But it was as a guitarist that his reputation echoed through Basil Spence's muted-modernist cloisters and leafy campus. He could hold his own in most company as a drummer, but guitar was the instrument he wove spells with. He was ever in demand for parties, Union Nights, whatever. And Paula had no mean way with the vocals, which was how they got together. After Sussex, he could have made a living as almost anything but he seemed to get by without sweat through knowing blokes who knew blokes and playing gigs.

Once, when they were students, he had taken Russell home with him. In the front room of the terraced house in North Paddington there was a big framed photograph of his parents on the dockside on their day of arrival in 1951, their faces youthfully shining, his father looking not yet grown into his trilby hat and baggy double-breasted suit. Midget Kingston stood between them. He had been named, of course, after the city from which they had embarked.

Kingston was laughing through most of the Test Match, just like he did much of the time when he was really on the cricket field. Somebody held a catch, somebody dropped a catch, he'd laugh. Same if he did either himself. Somebody banged a six, somebody got out, he'd laugh. Some fielder cut off a ball brilliantly on the boundary, or skidded calamitiously out of control, he'd laugh.

They never knew how it started. Camilla, Sarah and Russell had all had their noses in their work in other rooms, and only heard Paula's shriek and the sound of smashing.

As Russell got to the door of the kitchen, he saw Paula about to throw an empty jamjar at Kingston. He ducked and it disintegrated on the tiled floor where a bowl was shattered already. The honey-colour of his cricket bat had glinted in a corner of the kitchen since he'd casually propped it there several days before. He grabbed at it, deftly turned aside the mayonnaise jar that came next. It exploded against the Aga stove, and the splattered mayonnaise sizzled and burned. Then Russell's transistor radio got magnificently hooked through the kitchen window. Paula snatched it from its shelf, the voice which made music with him now just a screech. They had had to pay for that window afterwards.

Camilla put herself between them.

"Get out of the kitchen, Kingston!" Laughing, he backed out of the door into the garden.

Paula shoved Camilla aside, and charged out after him. By the side of the back door was a stack of garden junk, more or less rusty and useless. The tin watering-can leaked, but they had managed to use it a few times. Paula scooped it up and hurled it. Kingston had space now, and could put his talents properly to work. An agile little jig to position himself, an instinctive reflex. His bat connected with a resonant musical BONG and the can went wheeling up into the sky. Russell watched it arc against a stand of Constable cloud and begin to drop again. Down it came onto the cottage roof with a clang and clatter, bounced, slithered, and landed in the lilac tree.

Mike climbed up later and got it. He'd missed the Test Match because he'd gone for some interview. Russell thought they might have to pay for the damage to the tiles, but they were never charged.

While their eyes were off Paula, she had shot back inside and out again with Kingston's guitar. As the can was bounding down the roof she was already pounding his hundred or so quid's worth of music against the jagged Sussex flint of the cottage wall. She did it again and again, swinging the guitar so violently by its neck that no one could get close enough to grab her or it. Kingston had simply turned his back. He strolled with that light natural swagger of his to the bottom of the garden.

For a moment he seemed to stand contemplating the big old apple tree, his arms slightly spread at his sides, the bat handle in one hand, the other splayed loosely. He rested the bat tenderly against the trunk of the tree. Then he reached up and snapped off one of the hard unripe apples.

He was tossing it up and down in the palm of his hand, watching Paula manically swinging what was left of the guitar. Then he started polishing the apple on his jeans.

Christ, thought Russell, he's going to bowl it at her.

Russell had seen Kingston's fast bowling. He didn't care much for the game himself but a couple of times he'd watched the University XI for half-an-hour because Mike and Kingston had been playing. Mike, as you might expect where he came from, was the serious cricketer. Kingston just played, like he did a lot of things, with a kind of second nature, and got picked for the team sometimes. He could make a reckless pile of runs, when he managed to stay in, but he didn't get many wickets because he wasn't accurate, wasn't concentrated. But fast he was. He'd sometimes be brought on as a psychological weapon when the side was in need of one. And if often worked. He'd hit the man more often than the stumps, got warned plenty. Russell knew that if he let that hard apple fly and it struck, he could pretty nearly knock Paula's head off.

"Here, Kingston!" he called, loping over the grass towards him. He held out his hands. "Give me a catch!"

Kingston lobbed hard at him. Russell missed the catch of course. But the apple was gone, somewhere in the long grass of the meadow which came flush up against the garden's edge.

Kingston laughed again. He picked up the bat and strolled back towards Paula. She had stopped swinging, held the wreck of the guitar in one hand, and wailed. Then, a few yards from her, he dropped the bat on the grass.

"Oh, for fuck's sake, Paula, let's stop this shit."

But she'd darted for the bat. She lunged at him and caught him with a dead-sounding thump across the back. Russell got there and wrenched at the bat just as she was re-sighting it at Kingston's head. Sarah had got her tight round the waist, and Camilla caught both her hands.

Kingston walked down the side of the cottage, out onto the dirt track, and wasn't seen again for a week.

Paula's face, which for its sculpted lines someone had once called "classical", had fallen, as it were, into ruin, and her blonde hair was a haystack. She shook and shook, wouldn't stop, her body leaping with sobs. Her shin and one hand were bleeding where she'd slipped in the kitchen on the broken glass.

Camilla and Russell got her into the main room and locked the door, and Sarah ran to the phone by the bus-stop to call for help.

She was in hospital for months and never returned to university.

It was a hell of a job getting that burned-on mayonnaise off the Aga. They paid the outstanding rent and the bill for the damages. Actually, Paula's mother paid most of it. She didn't seem angry or to blame any of them for what had happened, even Kingston. Almost apologetic in fact, as if she was somehow responsible for her daughter having caused *them* the trouble. When Camilla phoned from the hospital to tell her, there was a long silence. When Camilla said: "Hallo, Mrs. Cleveley, are you still there?" her voice came back: "Sorry Camilla. I'll come down straight away."

Exactly that week later, as Russell was eating in the Union cafeteria, Kingston appeared out of nowhere. The seat opposite him had been empty, he had looked down at his plate; and when he looked up again there was Kingston.

"What you eating, man? Christ, *that* crap. I been home for some home cooking. That bitch Paula never could cook ...."

"She's *not* a bitch, Kingston."

"O.K., O.K. Sorry, sorry. But you know, some home nosh. Hang loose a bit. Some good jamming, I borrowed a guitar. Feel better now." Then he picked up a paper serviette from the table and slapped it with the splayed fingers of one hand across his face. He slowly lowered it to uncover his eyes, fixed on Russell, and said through the paper: "Stick by me, man."

Several months afterwards, Camilla went to see Paula. She was very calm. Kept wanting to touch Camilla too, quite demonstrably affectionate, which she never had been before. She'd always been a bit tense and prickly, or brooding and ebullient by turns. She couldn't talk to Camilla in any sustained way about the course they'd been doing together, or much else.

"Some doctor wanted to speak to me," Camilla told the others. "I just tried to answer his questions, what else could I do? They've used E.C.T. on her, would you believe it."

Russell said to Camilla now: "It was almost more like a war than a Test Match."

"But a war from long ago," said Camilla.

She sensed what he was going to say.

"Yes. But wars from long ago leave traces. Camilla, I still don't know what I feel about all that. How I feel about Kingston."

And she remembered how he sometimes used to say, wars just have to be got over. It's the only way after wars, it's no good perpetuating resentments. Now he says, wars leave traces. Both are right, of course. About some things he had always been right, more right than she was.

"But you *do* know not all was O.K. with Paula even before that. Maybe anybody could have set if off. I could tell, you know, from what her mother said, she'd always been half-expecting something like it. It was just that Kingston and she were the worst possible together."

Yes, Russell was a doubter and agoniser about everything, a non-truster. Yet, in an almost opposite way, he always *had* drawn the line in the sand, never made easy trade-offs. If he had a kind of vision of an impossible goodness and fullness, he had never substituted the specious for it. *He* could be trusted. She hadn't got to fear he had changed. She had found what she'd left behind, without even having to go back for it. She couldn't help feeling, well, honoured was a bit of a starchy word, but that *was* it, that he had held to her. Nothing had ever been more right than this, different as they were: *because* they were different.

It is the excellence most unlike our own that we will be most eager to acknowledge, since it not only extends but completes us. Randall Jarrell. Mary Sturgess had used that as the epigraph to one of her books.

"But Kingston was always particularly *your* friend," she said.

✳

If this were a fantasy it might draw to a close with Editha Wiegand struck by the couple sitting on the other side of a café in the Oranienburgerstrasse.

With Russell Hanslope noticing a woman – she wore a smart two-piece of expensive-looking greenish material and would have been about his own age – some tables away from Camilla and himself in a café in the Oranienburgerstrasse.

Editha is saying to herself, yes, that *could* be Russell. However much older he is, must be about *sechsig* now, like herself, that could be him. Grey now, but still all that lovely hair, nor nearly all gone like Gerhardt's.

Something about that woman, Russell is thinking, the way perhaps the lower lip drops in a hint of a smile, makes me think of Editha. Thought she was looking at me just now. Can't be sure, so many years ago, we must both look different, mustn't stare. Couldn't be her, of course, could be anywhere in Germany now, not even in Germany.

They are speaking English, aren't they, he and that woman he's with? Editha thinks she catches a few phrases even at the distance she is. She has learned a little since she knew Russell, mostly thanks to her children. All young people speak English now. Distinguished-looking woman. *Sicher, eine Frau im reiferen Alter*, like herself, but with the kind of marked presence certain women have at that age. Once or twice she's been told she has it herself. Naturally, Russell will have married years ago, like herself. Children? Grown up now, if there are some, like her own three.

A flicker of disquiet starts in her now as it always does when she thinks of her feelings when she married Gerhardt Wiegand in 1963. His was what her parents considered an offer she couldn't refuse. *He* was no *verflixter Fremder*, confounded foreigner without apparent prospects, you couldn't know anything about. Yes, he was a very nice young man, and very proper, and was in his father's business, and came to visit in a gleaming modern *Opel* which impressed her father. Yes, she *did* like him, rather in spite of her parents' pestering. But she could have refused the offer without batting an eyelid, *ohne mit der Wimper zu zucken*, if Russell had turned up at any time right until the moment of the ceremony. Of course, all those years with Gerhardt made a difference. Her children, naturally, were wonderful, quite wonderful. She wouldn't want anything, now, to be otherwise.

Really, nobody should want the past back.

Russell had finally got Camilla away, for a whole month. He'd been trying to get her to take a break for the best part of ten years, ever since they'd met again in '87. There'd been the odd few days here and there, but never this long. Yes, she'd say each time, she would love it, to both go somewhere for longer, but first there was this to do, then something else that couldn't be left. She'd given up her job now, but she had these consultancies still and was always being called on ....

It would have to be Berlin first, because she'd got these meetings set up with some people from the SPD there, but then they could go off wherever they felt like. The meetings would be in English, of course, but what a help it would be in Germany if Russell came along. She'd never gone *into* politics like at twenty-three she'd thought she might but she couldn't keep out of it either, especially at a moment like this. It had been a long, long time, and now Blair was going to win the election, Camilla was sure of it, probably be called in the spring next year. She was contributing to a project for Millbank.

"Had he been in Berlin before?" asked one of the Social Democrats. Camilla had introduced Russell to them in a bar after one of their sessions. "A long time ago. Before even the wall went up! I spent a few days here in fifty-seven." Use perfect tense in German. Odd to think of a tense being *perfect*, the only thing in this world that is, Camilla would say. Of course, they don't have a perfect *continuous* like in English. "*I have been spending a few days in Berlin ....*" More logical than us. A perfect moment, maybe, but the *continuous* perfect? Continuous *im*perfect, more like. But then, if you asked these Berliners, is the past continuous, what would they say?

Böll addressed that question again and again. It was there even in such a single lean sentence as "*In den Jahren 1939 bis 1945 hatten wir Krieg.*"

But the old myths had to be exploded, another Social Democrat said, the old nationalist myths, the old myths about Germany including the ones the English liked to cling on to, even the old socialist myths. The man's English was good, he used that English idiom, to Camilla. How would you say that in German? You "lay against" something, Russell seemed to recall.

And Russell could hear Camilla building an adroit answer about yes, that's very true, very necessary, but at the same time you have to go on drawing the line in the same place in the sand.

But somehow, to talk, in Berlin, about explosions ....

Then, on that earlier visit, as he'd taken in the glinting steel and glass of the *Wirtschaftswunder*, Russell had thought of Auden's line about "New styles of architecture, a change of heart." His mother had been fond of saying that his father must have bombed Berlin, good thing too, give Hitler a taste of his own medicine. But there was that day, near the end of the war, after the telegram about his father, impossible to remember exactly how long after, when Mrs. Machin had come to see them. Sal, as his mother always called her. He recalled her clearly enough, with her little utility hat cocked slightly sideways, and the dealing-with-children tone of voice in which she said she didn't think your daddy went on bombing raids. It had been some other special thing when he'd been shot down. Secret, probably, anyway Uncle Reg wouldn't tell her about it. His mother and her old friend had gone into the sitting-room for a long time. He had kicked around the house, scattered his sister Meg's crayons. He couldn't settle, with those sounds of voices he could just hear through the sitting-room door. Yes, he was only seven, but something was all wrong, he could tell. His mother held her handkerchief and hid her eyes when the two women appeared again.

He didn't think his mother ever saw much of her friend Sal after that. The Machins had gradually come to live in a different world to a hard-up widow like her.

That woman over there in the smart green outfit was no more than some shadow or similitude of Editha, he was pretty sure, but she served a purpose, she served as a left trace of what, though in the past tense, was indeed a reality. Real life, as he had then thought. Wherever Editha actually was she'd have grown-up children now. She'd not know that *he'd* never had any. There were Camilla's son and daughter, of course. Marvellous. One afternoon when Mary had called, Mary named after Mary Sturgess who had died a couple of years ago and left Camilla the original typescripts of her eight books, he'd watched her talking nineteen-to-the-dozen to her mother, her ear-lobe loaded with rings, her hair cropped short round her head, some kind of little tattoo on her shoulder, when she slipped her denim jacket off. She'd been to Boston to see her father, both the kids loved it over there. So there was a lot to talk about. Every now and then she'd incline her head towards him and say: "I'm right, aren't I Russell?" or "*You* know what I mean, don't you?" Good to have him there as a foil to her mother. Also, she knew her mother so well, she could see plainly something added to her since Russell had been around. She hadn't been able to stop herself coming out to her father one day with what she was a little afraid may have sounded schoolgirlishly wet: "I think Mum's really in love. I never saw her like it before."

The anonymous woman in expensive green, who by the law of random distribution not wholly implausibly *is* Editha, watches as the Englishman speaks to the waiter in German, and the Englishwoman smiles, and they get up from their table. The sounds of a reunited Berlin, with its skyline of countless semaphoring cranes, come in through the door as they go out. Here they are in what not long since was the no-go, walled-off East, and they feel as easy as in London. It does not mean that all, everywhere, is well, any more than it was when Russell nearly fifty years ago had been troubled by the "thoughts" he wrote in his notebook.

It does mean, Camilla says, that things never have to stay the way they were. That nothing's a forlorn hope …

Recalling young Mary in the apartment that day, bobbing up and down from her seat, rummaging around the room picking up this thing and that, often marked with some childhood moment, looking each over rapidly, making some remark, unable to keep still for long, "What's the perfect tense to *her*?" Russell suddenly thinks. "Continuous or otherwise. Her head's full of the imperfect, oh-so-urgent now. She's *not* just like her mother at that age, when we were at Sussex, of course, that tired old nostalgic reduction. But still …."

Nothing is finished

White

"Everything white, every stone, every roof, all the ways, the lamps, each tree and bush. And you know, of course, how wonderful I find snow, how deeply, satisfyingly good it makes me feel."

It's many years ago now that my friend Luisa wrote that to me. The postmark is still there, on the envelope lightly freckled with age. It brings back to me the small town of W—— where she lived. The place lies among low hills, though much of the country in those parts is flat plain, between Cologne and the Dutch border. But the mildly lyrical vein in which she had opened her letter gradually subsided into a brown study.

"Then, as I stomped through the woods, I began to ask myself, what precisely is this satisfaction? What precisely in the world around one is it that touches one so deeply?"

She knew that I was still in touch with Hayden. Hayden and I had met her in Cologne when we were sent for a few months there by our office. We were both very young, still struggling to get on the career ladder, though as it happened, neither of us ever did climb that particular ladder. Hayden, indeed, eventually became an art historian of some standing. In fact, more than any putative career opportunities, what interested us both was the taste of life which a city like Cologne could offer, something different from what seemed to us the dreariness of Leicester as it was in the late nineteen-fifties. And quite naturally, our interest centred upon the *Fräulein*. I don't remember precisely how we met Luisa. I believe we were at the Philharmonic Hall one evening, and by what with him was a sort of reflex action, Hayden chatted her up in the scramble for drinks during the interval. I think he effected one of his favourite stratagems, that of knocking lightly against her in the crush, and spilling a few drops from her glass, whereupon apologies followed. That may have been Luisa, or it may have been another of the several *Fräulein* he assailed during our stay. In any case, we began to meet her quite regularly. Sometimes she brought along her friend Petra, with whom I walked sedately hand-in-hand during our saunters through the wooded countryside around W——. Hayden and Luisa occasionally disappeared into the trees, leaving Petra and me to make small-talk in my stilted German or her broken English.

I do indeed remember two or three such walks after heavy snowfalls when the woods took on a quite phantasmal beauty.

I broached at least once with Hayden the question of what he was "up to" with Luisa. Wasn't she perhaps beginning to read a bit more into things than he intended? He waved the question away. Surely I didn't believe he would let himself get dragged into something with a local girl when we were here so briefly? Did I think he couldn't foresee all the problems that would entail? Or that he would deliberately mislead her? Didn't I know him better than that?

Well, yes, I thought, I did know him a bit, and that was just the worry.

She went on writing to *me* for three or four years, long after Hayden had dropped her. And here's this particular letter, which has turned up in some old papers.

"There is some unfathomable mystery in it all. In winter as a sharp foil to the sweetness of summer. And looking out over the cold restful stillness of a winter landscape, the bare trees seem to me somehow seen dimly, through a fog, even when there is none. They look as if they are sleeping and waiting. It seems given to the trees to wait out winter and in that waiting gather powers for the time of new growth, new spring. Am I, then, sleeping and waiting?"

Not long after we returned to Leicester, Hayden gave in his notice at the office and went off to do his Art History degree. His first university Christmas vacation was spent back in Cologne, and it was at that time, I believe, that promises were made – vows exchanged, if one might put it so antiquatedly. It had, of course, snowed. He went back at least a couple more times, ostensibly studying the Wallraf-Richartz collection. And indeed, he did some years later publish a strangely, compellingly, meditative essay on that collection.

Vows and promises. Most of her letters to me ended on the same note:

"Only my spring is over and there is a great emptiness in me. I find no connections any more. When, anyway, does living begin? With the first cry? With the first poem? Does it begin with the first kiss, with the first heartbreak? With the first success? In the moment of holding one's first child? How can anyone be able to count the stations of a life? *My living began with his love coming into my life. How will it end?*

"I'll finish now because here come my visitors tapping on the door, stamping for warmth on the path outside, and I must come to the surface and do that kind of living, that surface kind of living, which is immeasurably hard, because I must have the other living in order to bear living at all. Petra is among them and she will ask after you. Her fiancé, a schoolteacher from Aachen, is with her."

*

In early December, the first day to feel truly like winter, sharp-etched white cloud climbing over the tower-blocks, the Wren spires, his great dome and over moderate foot-traffic on the bright aluminium blade of the Millennium Bridge, I went to the Barnett Newman exhibition at the Tate Modern. Hayden, with whom, after a break of something like thirty years during which we hardly communicated, my friendship had in recent years resumed, had especially recommended it to me. I shall relate my encounter with Newman's work in some detail because it seemed to take its place in a larger narrative of encounters. I had first to run the gauntlet, dumb down as if with an aspirin the ache it induced in me, of Anish Kapoor's monstrous triple-trumpet installation which had so ruthlessly appropriated the great expanse of the Turbine Hall. This sculpture, called Marsyas, constructed in red PVC which perhaps echoes the flayed flesh of Apollo's victim, had received much praise. It had been compared to the fan-vaulting of a vast cathedral. Its membrane had been described as ever-shifting in texture as one moves along it, ever mutating according to the light. It had been said to activate and fill the cavernous space of Herzog and de Meuron's post-industrial interior. I have observed Kapoor's work before and derived mild entertainment from its precisely engineered effects. This, though, was a monstrous oppressor, an abuse to this space the power of which flows from its sensorily and psychically elusive capaciousness. It darkened and confined a space which normally excites with its amplitude and openness to light. I endured the ordeal and travelled the escalators to the fourth level.

The American abstract painter Barnett Newman did not begin making his significant work until he was into his forties. He was born of Polish-Jewish immigrants in New York in 1905 and in 1933 had offered himself as a candidate for mayor of New York City on a programme of "action by men of culture". How many votes he got is not recorded. The war in Europe was a watershed for his development. He said: "When Hitler was ravaging Europe, could we express ourselves by having a beautiful girl lying naked on a divan?" And again: "I felt the issue in those years was – what can a painter do?" No work in the exhibition dated from before 1944. The earliest works on show were crayon and brush-and-ink drawings from 1944–5, in which the move toward abstraction has not yet dispensed with organic forms, sprouting and spiralling, which seemed to echo some of the devices and mannerisms of the Surrealist painters of the thirties. Nevertheless, I did not feel myself in the presence of an artist at all deeply committed to that kind of programme; rather, what immediately struck me, gathered me, as it were, into a sympathetic attunement the opposite of my alienation from the Kapoor beyond these galleries, was the way colour, form and line work as nuanced and sensitively human "embodiments of feeling", to use Newman's own phrase. That, as I moved on and encountered the increasing austerity of Newman's means, and the intensity this generated, as he voyaged into an almost total abstractionism, became ever more manifest.

"I think a man spends his whole lifetime painting one picture or working on one piece of sculpture,' Newman said in 1950. He seemed seeking to construct a continuous coherent narrative. Yet he also suggested that each picture offered a distinct, unrepeated experience. Yes, I could see how the same visual motifs, the same experiential phenomena, were being reworked, re-engaged with, reenvisaged, in each painting, and yet each picture presented me with a new field of gravity, sensory and meditative. I have similar responses to Rothko, some of whose work hangs elsewhere in the Tate Modern, though mistakenly in a walk-through room in a way that I feel Rothko himself would have disapproved. Those works should be enclosed in an hermetic space, as indeed they were when they hung in the old Tate Gallery at Millbank. One should not be constantly distracted by a procession of visitors sauntering through, with varying degrees of interest, to other exhibits. Here, in the Barnett Newman exhibition, there was generally room to experience the works uninterrupted. And they are different from Rothko's; where his fields of colour interact and their edges shimmer and shift unfixedly, Newman was developing something of what came to be hard-edged abstractionism, though at times he did permit his geometrical boundaries to waver. Clean lines, streamlining, industrial materials held their attraction for him. But he did not seem seduced by the industrial-technological ethos. That was not what visual abstraction meant for him. Each work is a humanist statement. The exhibition leaflet pointed out that Newman often compared the "visual experience of the painting" to an "encounter with a person, a living being." Somewhere – *Time Out* I think – wrote complainingly of Newman's portentous pronouncements on his own work, and recommended setting these aside before one could properly engage with the art. Well, perhaps an artist should not always be nudging his audience. But this life-long dialogue, I thought, between the maker of the work and the work itself reveals an artist profoundly engaging with his project, ever wrestling with what being a maker involves, breaking new possibilities out of his medium, seeking to inscribe that coherent narrative. The result is a cerebral art, yes, but a process of cerebration which deepens and enhances, and which is never, remarkably, at the expense of the sensuous and emotional qualities of the works one is witnessing. "The self, terrible and constant, is for me the subject matter of painting", he wrote. We are presently in the trammels of a postmodern orthodoxy which proclaims both narrative and selfhood moveable feasts, finally indeterminable and unknowable. One may take the force of that. Yet one feels on the pulse that such a perception occupies at best a kind of parallel universe to that of how or for what we live. For me there remained, occurring between oneself as viewer and the painting that manifested itself before one, something indefeasible, something which answered to my own story: that terrible reality of selfhood, and of interaction between selfhoods.

Newman's finest works, perhaps, are his *Stations of the Cross*, in relation to which he said that he conceived of Christ's passion as having become "the cry of man, of every man". This son of a Jewish immigrant, various of whose works draw on Jewish creation-myth and ritual of Atonement, felt, he said, that Christ's single moment in which he cried out "why have you forsaken me" had become in the twentieth century a universal cry. The large gallery in which these hung seemed, as one walked into it, immersed in light. The pain of the century, of the aftermath of wars, uttered in paint as a tortured cry by such as Pollock, is not so represented by Newman. He actualizes it in a measured assemblage of inventions, no longer meticulously hard-edged, running through many gradations of white and culminating in a supernumerary fifteenth station of ultimate whiteness. Of these "stations" he said: "I wished no monuments, no cathedrals. I wanted a human scale for the human cry."

I encountered here what I have encountered elsewhere – in the work of Käthe Kollwitz in Cologne and Berlin, to take a notable example, though but one among others: an exemplification of that for which the aesthetic seems peculiarly just and enabled, while tenacious of its own terms, to speak of the unbearable, to take upon its shoulders the anguish and the enormities of such a century as has recently passed.

*

These reflections, more or less, I delivered to Hayden when I met him shortly afterwards, as we'd arranged, in a tiny pub we knew in Brighton Kemp Town.

He listened indulgently to my no doubt half-baked layman's recital. But something more was on my mind. That and Hayden and my thoughts about my visit to the Tate Modern a week or two before seemed to have knitted themselves together.

I rediscovered Luisa's letter when I was hunting out bits and pieces – pamphlets, museum guides, photos and whatnot – which I'd hoarded from that time in Cologne. What perhaps had become a bit of an obsession for me over the years had been compounded by a recent reading of Bernhard Schlink's *Der Vorleser*. This book had seemed to raise more questions than it helped answer. It provoked naggings which were duly appended to a stack of notes I'd accumulated. And then I'd started pondering whether I should show Luisa's letter to Hayden.

Would it seem I was confronting him with some sort of reproach? Surely not, after all this time, and the lives we'd been overtaken by, had gone on to fashion. No, what it comes down to is that as time passes the need for a coherent narrative, for seeing how each part fits, seems more and more to press. That's why, presumably, leaving aside the ghosted trash of so-called celebrities who only have their sights on the wallow of ever more publicity and lucre, people write memoirs and autobiographies. Despite, or even because of, the elusive, shifting ghost-worlds our subjectivities occupy, despite the acknowledgement that one never can see it whole, one wants to work away at it as Newman did. A pretty transitory and minor affair, no doubt, that brief interinvolving of Hayden and myself and Luisa. Yet there it was, a resistant, occasionally troubling, knot in the narrative, touching that terrible reality of selfhood and of interaction of selfhoods of which Barnett Newman had felt his paintings spoke. Showing Hayden the letter was becoming a compulsion.

The envelope with its faint foxing rustled a bit as I took it out of my bag. The envelopes Luisa used, containing an inner layer of a kind of grey rice-paper, had always done that. Hayden glanced at it and noticed, I think, the German stamps – President Heuss, wasn't it? – perhaps also the handwriting. Then he looked sideways, half-smiling, hard at me. No doubt he was thinking: "What the hell is *this* about?"

But he took the letter from the envelope and read absorbedly. A few regulars dropped in or drifted off, most giving out that air of mild theatricality with which it sometimes seems the Brighton ether is infused and which seeps into its inhabitants. The two or three women louche and exaggerated, a populace of mysterious occupation and sources of income despite, often, ostensibly careless yet artfully assembled get-ups from probably expensive shops. A couple of second-hand dealers from the *boutiques* with freakish new-age names along the street. Two gents *d'un certain age* propped on stools at the bar, one delivering in the meant-to-be-overheard tones of the pub bore an account of the tribulations which had attended the preparation of his boat at the marina for putting to sea. I rather doubted whether the lure of the ocean would ever win out over that of the barstool.

Hayden drank his beer quietly and I went and got us two more. A tiny woman in some kind of purple cloak shuffled past us, her face plastered with make-up like a stage-mask and crooked so that one side seemed to hang lower than the other, only sandals on her blue swollen feet though the temperature outside was barely above freezing. The woman behind the bar – "Hello, Miriam love, how's your luck to-day?" "Don't ask" – poured her something into a small glass without having to ask what. Hayden watched her absently.

"Daily tipple's probably all that keeps her going," he muttered to me. He'd read the letter through. "Yes", he said, looking down at it again. "Yes. Don't think I've forgotten all that. I think of it often. If only for a few seconds."

Then he held the sheets of notepaper out in front of me, smiling again.

"So what prompted *this* disinterment of ancient history?"

"Well look. 'Everything white.'" I waved a finger over the opening sentences. "Well, I don't know, this may sound a bit fantastical. When I came into that space with the Newman *Stations of the Cross*, the light in there and the whiteness. And *then* that phrase of hers about the stations of life."

We both contemplated our glasses.

"And those questions, 'When, anyway, does living begin?' and all that. Rhetorical, I know. *He* wanted to paint the human cry, he said."

"She was thinking of herself, you know. She was a very introspective girl, even if ... reaching out for something more."

"On a human scale. She was pretty upset."

"Upsets, upsets. We live with them. You know I got into that business with Imogen at the university. Her tutorials were good, the timetabled ones, I mean. The ones in her bed better. Oh yes, disbelieve it if you like, we thrashed out issues in art then too. You knew enough stuff about my life at that time." He paused, revolving his glass on our table as it caught the light. "Look! That amber glow ...."

"Lovely," I said.

"In the end I made a judgement. I don't know how, I don't know why. Don't ask me, I just don't know any more. I decided it didn't make sense. How do you handle that without upset? I wish someone, you or anyone, had told me how. Anyway, I just dropped her. Never heard from her again."

She had continued writing to *me* though, the letters becoming more and more desolate, even after I myself had rather got out of touch with Hayden.

"Even after she got married," I said. "She wrote she was getting married, but could we still write to each other at least once a year. And we did, for the first couple of years. She didn't say a lot about the husband."

But there'd never been any mistaking the sub-text of those letters. And then I just got too busy and was too far away, and we stopped the letters.

"I might have written my books in German. Who knows, who knows."

And he stared pensively again over at the purple-shrouded mini-woman sipping at her glass .... "And the bloody bloke still hasn't come ... crappy workmen .... Here!" Pushing her glass to the edge of her rickety table. "That one's lonely. Give us another."

Hayden started to say something else but then the door to the street opened. Hayden's daughter stood outlined against the light for a moment, then came towards us.

"*Look* at you two old degenerates." And she flicked her eyes upwards. "Soaking in that shit up on the ceiling, too, I bet."

The pub's claim to fame, apart from its micro-dimensions and the quality of its micro-brewed ale, was the Edwardian nude photographs pasted every-which-way across the ceiling.

Hayden gave her a hug and I gave her the sort of peck on the cheek nowadays *de rigueur*. I'd met Petra a few times before and rather taken to her mix of assertiveness and daughterly dependence, despite that rehearsed down-market manner young people often have nowadays. Petra was in Brighton negotiating a show of some of her own installation works at the Brighton festival. She was taking her father off to meet somebody or other, for his advice, or at least moral support. We drank up.

It was getting late-afternoonish when we eventually emerged. "Newman ... one or two things ...." Hayden said, turning his head as he and Petra walked away. "We must talk again". I went down past the tall, narrow Victorian terrace-house in which my father-in-law had been born, at the tail-end of the nineteenth century, within view of the sea.

There was a light sprinkling of snow over the pebbles on the beach. I remembered before I'd known Hayden, or Luisa, going down onto the pebbles on some beach one day in a sprinkling of snow like this with some girl and looking out to a lightly reddening late-afternoon horizon, and wondering ....

When, anyway, did living begin? But after all, didn't *that* seem an odd question.

And of course the horizon always recedes, a simple enough notion, ever another beyond, always another beginning. Looked at in a certain way, that couplet of Blake's that had long stuck in my mind might make a kind of sense:

And every thing exists and not one sigh nor smile nor tear
One hair nor particle of dust, not one can pass away.

Of course, he meant in a domain other than that of the fallen material "nature" he scorned and abhorred.

I've seen it recently asked by some wind-up, finger-on-the-popular-pulse TV critic, can there be anything more to say about World War II, the bombing, the landings, the Holocaust, and all that stuff?

Maybe not. But Blake was right, nothing can pass away. And some things can only be said over and over again.